Pre   ،u Epic Calling.

By
Andrew Dobell

The book is Copyright © to Andrew Dobell, Creative Edge Studios Ltd, 2019.
No part of this book may be reproduced without prior permission of the
copyright holder.

All locations, events, and characters within this book are either fictitious, or
have been fictionalised for the purposes of this book.

Welcome to the Magi Saga

This is book one of a long, sprawling adventure over several series of books, of which, this is the start.

This book has been through various editions, with this being the latest.

I hope you enjoy reading about the adventures of Amanda and the Magi, as much as I have enjoyed writing them.

Acknowledgements

For my Grandfather, who was a continual inspiration and support. I miss you, and this is for you.

Thank you to my wife and family for their love and tolerance and help. You make everything worthwhile.

Thank you to my old gaming friends, you guys have inspired this story more than you can know. I have some of the best memories from those hours sitting at the gaming table.

Thank you to my Editors Julie Hall, CP Bialois, and Hanna Elizabeth. Your input has been amazing, thank you.

Thank you to Vicki Blatchley for being my cover model.

Dedication
For my boys, my kids, I love you!

Language
I'm a British author living in Britain, and I write in British English with British spellings.   ;-)

Booklist

For full list of Andrew Dobells Books, visit his website at;
http://www.andrewdobellauthor.co.uk/booklist

Table of Contents

Welcome to the Magi Saga 2
Acknowledgements 2
Booklist 2
Table of Contents 3
Amanda-Jane Page 4
Prologue 5
Epiphany 6
The Inquisitor 14
A chance meeting 20
Revelation 28
Acquisition 35
Investigation 40
Apprenticeship 45
Visits 52
Body and Spirit 58
Angel 64
Orphanage 70
Broken 77
Legacy 82
Blood Bath 97
Ball 102
Escape 109
Dig 115
Liberation 121
Boarding Action 130
Moving on 141
Epilogue 143
Booklist 146

Amanda-Jane Page

By
Adam Hughes
http://www.justsayah.com/

Prologue

Cairo, Egypt

Irfan ran through the streets of Cairo, his heart pounding, his adrenalin pumping. Everything was making him jump. Every shadow in the night seemed like it was another monster about to attack him, drag him down a dark alleyway, and eat him alive.

He'd been like this for the last few days as he'd rode hard through the desert to get away from… He didn't know what it was he was trying to escape, but he'd seen it. That thing. That monster, that demon. He'd seen what it had done, and now he just wanted to get away.

He'd sold that damn tablet he'd found at the camp. He felt sure it was cursed. The market trader he'd sold it to had just laughed at him and made some comment about amateur tomb raiders or something.

Irfan didn't care what the trader said. He knew what he'd seen, and he didn't ever want to see it again.

But tonight, wandering through the dark streets, past shadowy people, his nerves had gotten the better of him. He saw danger and monsters everywhere, and in that last alleyway, something had grabbed his leg. He was sure of it, and that was the final straw.

He ran around a corner and saw one of the city's Catholic churches. There, he thought, no demon would follow him in there. Irfan ran and crashed through the door, only to stumble and fall to the mosaic floor. He groaned in pain.

"My son," said a friendly male voice. "What seems to be the problem?"

Irfan looked up to see a priest standing beside him, looking down with concern etched into the lines of his face.

"Oh, thank God. Please, you have to help me. The demon, it's after me, I'm sure of it. Please... Please..." he sobbed, tears running down his cheeks.

"Demon?" the priest asked.

"Yes, the demon with the bighorn. It's coming, Father. It's going to kill me! Please, can you help?"

Epiphany

Manhattan, New York

Walking towards the entrance of the alleyway, the man in front of her looked back and smiled. "Thanks," he said, looking sheepish and slightly embarrassed.

"No, thank you," she replied with a wink and a smile, as she stuffed the small stack of bills into her bag.

The man, who she knew only as Rorie, looked away and turned back to the street. He caught the eye of Stuart stood a short distance away and nodded once before striking out into the night. Stuart looked over at her with a questioning look on his face. Amanda smiled and nodded once back to him, signalling that everything was okay.

Looking back at her john as he walked up the street, a small part of her knew she would miss him just a little bit. Amanda had been making money like this for a little over a year now, coming out to these streets, meeting men who were looking for some affection, a fleeting encounter, or just some kind of release.

She didn't get much enjoyment out of their encounters, she just went through the motions and usually, only did what was needed to get paid. It wasn't like she'd had much choice in the matter, her options had been limited. She did have a few regulars though, men she'd come to know, lonely men who came to her for some kindness, for a human connection. Rorie was one of them. She felt sorry for him really and would try to give him what he needed. When she'd first started, she never would have believed that she'd end up caring for some of her johns.

Her clients were only human, though, with human needs and desires.

She'd toyed with telling these men that she was moving on, that she'd no longer be here, waiting for them, in a few days. Stuart had advised against it though, saying it was dangerous, there was no telling how some of them might react.

He was right.

Instead, she gave a little more of herself, a little more affection, a little more time, and a greater connection as a kind of farewell gift.

"Are you okay?" Stuart asked.

"I'm grand," she answered in her Irish brogue. "I'm just wondering what Rorie will do when he realises I'm gone."

"Mandy, he's just a john. He'll be fine. You have more important things to worry about," Stuart replied, looking into her eyes from under his ever-present cap.

"Yeah, I know."

"You care too much, Mandy, you really do."

"You'll miss me when I'm gone, so yeh will." She smiled back at him, rubbing her neck. An alleyway was never a great place to have a fumble.

"I've got the other girls, I'll be fine. You need to be with Georgie anyway. She needs you more than I do right now. Has your passport come through yet?"

"It did, it came through the other day," she smiled.

"How is it? Did my man do a good job?"

"It looks real to me. He said it'll get me through customs, God love him. So fingers crossed, yeh know? I was able to book the flight with it already, though, so as long as they're not waiting for me at the airport, I think I'll be grand."

"I told you he does good work," Stuart said. "So, you fly tomorrow?"

"Day after. I'll pack tomorrow. I just can't wait to get out there. She's really sick, you know. They reckon any day now…" she said, her words catching in her throat at the thought of her friend. Tears welled up as she felt the emotional pain rise up again. She fought it back down, though, getting a grip on herself.

"Don't worry, she'll be waiting for you. I know she will. She wants to see her 'lucky charm' again, you'll see," he said. "You just get out there as quick as you can. You'll let me know when you arrive, won't you?"

"Of course," she said, smiling at Stuart's use of Georgina's nickname for her and the fake-sounding Irish accent he put on as he said it. It didn't even vaguely resemble the terrible accent of the leprechaun in the commercials, let alone a real Irish accent like hers.

"So, are you done for the night? You don't need to be out here, you know," he asked.

"No. I want to stay out a bit longer. Maybe one last trick?"

"Sure," he said as he pulled out his phone which was buzzing in his hand. He answered it, stepping away. Amanda watched him walk off before she looked down at herself. Her clothes were pulled out of shape, so she went over to the darkened window of a nearby shop and studied her reflection.

She stood around five-foot-six, not including the heels she wore tonight, and as usual when she was working the streets, she wore a short mini skirt and fitted top to 'show off the goods' to potential johns. She was slim, toned, and quite a buxom girl, making her one of Stuart's busier ladies. Tonight, she wore a denim jacket over her thin black-lace top to keep from getting too chilled. After smoothing down her clothing, re-adjusting herself, and reapplying her lipstick she ran her fingers through her long, red hair. It was a strong, saturated red, a deep burgundy crimson. People often asked her where she got the dye, but she'd never dyed it in her life. She'd hated it growing up, as it made her stand out, marked her as different, but now, she kind of liked it.

Georgina had called her pretty on many occasions, but Amanda wasn't convinced about that. It was probably the illness talking.

She stepped back from the window as Stuart approached her again and smiled.

"You look gorgeous as always, Red," he said.

"You charmer. What are you after?" she asked.

He laughed. "Nothing," he replied innocently.

"I bet," she replied with mock suspicion. "I'm gonna go get myself a drink from the shop, you want one?" she asked.

"No, I'm good. Here…" he said, stepping towards her and reaching for something in his pocket. He pulled out a stack of bills and flipped a few out. "Here, take this. I won't take it out of your share; the drink's on me," he said with a grin.

"Aww, thank you. I won't be a minute," she said.

"I'll be over with the others," he said, pointing over in the direction of four girls a little further up the sidewalk.

Amanda smiled, nodded, and turned to walk up the street. She was lucky, really lucky, to have Stuart out here protecting them. She hated the word pimp, even though that's what he was. She thought of him more as their protector or bodyguard than anything else. She knew she'd miss him when she left, but she also knew she didn't want to do this anymore. Working the streets had served a purpose, it was a means to an end and that was all. It wasn't as if it was her dream job or anything; she didn't enjoy it. She was the lowest of the low in most people's eyes, but she didn't care. They didn't know what she'd been through, and they never would.

She had regrets, sure. She wished she could have done something else, but this had been instant money when she'd needed it the most, and once she was doing it, it became harder and harder to walk away.

Georgina's illness and the surprise inheritance had finally changed all that.

She'd get herself a drink and head back to Stuart and see how the rest of the night went. She looked back and saw Stuart walk over to the rest of his girls not too far away. Jade was the oldest, then Jenny, Naomi, and Renee who was the youngest of them. They welcomed him as he stepped up to them.

As she watched, Stuart glanced back at her. She smiled. He was still as protective as ever, she thought.

Continuing on her way, she lost herself in thoughts of what clothes she would pack and take with her to Ireland when she left in two days. As she walked past the next alleyway along, something large and dark shot out from the shadows and wrapped around her, pinning her arms to her sides and crushing her body. The force of the grip compressed her ribcage and pressed the air out of her lungs. The moment it had her, the dark shape yanked her into the alleyway, whipping her head to the side with the sudden movement.

And then it let go of her, and she was flying along the alley. Weightless for a second, Amanda watched as the concrete below her whipped past, and then rose up to meet her.

Amanda hit the ground hard. It bit into her skin, spinning her around, and suddenly she was rolling sideways, splashing through puddles of dirty water, getting bashed and bruised as she went.

Without warning, a brick wall brought her to a bone-crunching stop as she banged her head against it and she rolled back, face down into a puddle.

"Ugh," Amanda groaned as a hundred cuts and scrapes that covered her body screamed for her attention. Placing her hands on the ground in the shallow puddle, she pushed herself up, hissing at the pain. Her lank hair fell about her face into the water that rippled with the drips that fell from her body.

What the hell had just happened? she wondered, as she got a leg beneath her and sat herself up.

A deep bass growl and the dull thuds of something big stalking towards her broke through the fog of pain and confusion. Amanda looked up and straight into the face of a nightmare.

Silhouetted against the comparatively bright main street, a huge black figure, easily twice the height of an ordinary man, stepped nimbly towards her. It looked human in basic shape, except enormous, and... furry?

Thinking her eyes were deceiving her, Amanda blinked, but the horrific vision didn't go away. The creature looked like it was made of muscle—layers and layers of it—beneath pitch-black skin covered in patches of matted sable hair. But that wasn't the worst of it. As it stepped into a weak light cast by the glow of a lone, bare light bulb hanging over a back entrance to one of the shops along the alley, the thing's inhuman face came into view.

It looked bat-like with its enormous ears, but that's where the similarity ended. Two huge tusks sprouted from its wide, drooling maw and a long, cancerous-looking horn jutted from its forehead.

Amanda's eyes went as wide as dinner plates and she scrambled back along the ground, trying to get away from it, only to hit the wall. This wasn't real. This couldn't be real. It was impossible.

'Where are you going, Witch?' The thing rumbled. Its voice was like thunder.

'What? What the fuck... shite, what do you want?' Amanda stammered as panic rose up within her. There was no way she could be calm and logical about this. Being attacked by a man was one thing, being assaulted by an impossible creature that shouldn't exist was something else entirely. Her heart was pounding like a drum in her chest, like it was about to burst forth and make a run for it. This had to be a nightmare of some kind. It was the only explanation. Things like this just didn't exist.

"Amanda!" called a voice from the street as Stuart sprinted around the corner. The creature turned and looked. It was as if Stuart didn't quite register what was stood before him—like his brain couldn't quite comprehend what it was as he ran towards her, only to come to a skidding stop right next to it as he realised the size of the thing.

"Holy shit!" Stuart called as he looked up at the creature and stepped back from it. With a lazy movement of its colossal arm, the thing slapped Stuart backwards into the wall. Amanda heard the crack of bone as his head hit the concrete.

"Stuart," Amanda called. "Run!"

Stuart looked up at her and touched his fingers to the back of his head. They came away a glistening crimson.

"Stuart," Amanda called again, only for the creature to pull back its fist, and as Stuart looked up at it, the thing punched him.

The creature's fist was as big as Stuart and ended up buried a few feet into the now-ruined concrete ground and wall of the building, with Amanda's friend crushed beneath it. The beast withdrew its fist from the rubble. Amanda noted the bloodstain that covered it as more debris fell on top of whatever remained of Stuart.

"You won't best me again, Witch. This time, you will pay," the thing growled at her. Amanda had no idea what it was talking about, and honestly, wasn't paying much attention. Instead, a single thought ran through her mind, over and over.

I'm gonna die, I'm gonna die, I'm gonna die…

The creature lowered itself into a more threatening pose, its claws held wide as it looked at her.

Panic and fear filled her up and bubbled over as she took in the scene, followed swiftly by rage. A wave of growing anger passed over her as she looked at the rubble that covered Stuart's body.

The fear she had been feeling was washed away by a growing white-hot fury as she thought about the events of the past few months. Her life was pretty shitty.

She'd come to America as a stowaway looking for a new life. Looking for hope. She'd convinced herself that her life and her future were here. Instead, she'd ended up on the street—cold, hungry, and alone. Even the pity of strangers hadn't saved her, and before long, she was turning tricks in the alleyways of Manhattan, dodging the cops and the gangs as she tried to make a life for herself, however meagre it may be.

She might tell anyone who asked that she liked her work, but the brutally honest truth of it was that she hated it. It made her feel used and abused. She was a thing, a sex object, and frankly, it was shit.

The money helped, but this wasn't the life she wanted, this wasn't the life she'd hoped for. But what else was there? She was stuck.

Her life sucked and if that wasn't enough, now fate was taking her friends from her as well. Georgina's illness, and now this thing from one of the darkest corners of Hell had just killed Stuart.

She clenched her fists over and over again as her breathing sped up, riding the wave of hot fury inside her. She wanted to lash out. She wanted to kill it. To tear it apart limb from limb, screaming in defiance at the hand she'd been dealt.

Her rage built to a crescendo as the creature lunged, rushing forward with its sword-like claws slicing at her. Amanda held her arms out in front of her, palms facing the creature, fingertips pointing to the sky in a futile effort to protect herself and screamed with all her might, releasing that rage and throwing it at the creature.

It felt like a wave of energy exploded out of her, rushing along her arms and out of her palms. An almighty crash and explosion rocked the alley, and even though her eyes were closed, she could make out a flare of white light beyond her eyelids.

The anticipated feeling of ten-inch claws ripping into her flesh never happened, and as the sense of rippling energy continued to flow over her arms, accompanied by hissing, banging, and flashes of light, Amanda opened her eyes.

Electrical energy in the form of huge arcs of blinding light flowed down her arms and shot out at the beast that stood before her, blasting it in the chest. The energy leapt about in great electrical arcs with branches slamming into walls and puddles, evaporating them with an explosion of steam. The rush of air kicked up papers and trash that were burnt by the energy as they wheeled about before her.

The creature staggered, struggling to keep its balance as Amanda gazed in awe at the power that was flowing out of her. Was there golden mist hanging in the air around her, as well? As she watched, her concern grew, accompanied by a healthy dose of doubt. To her dismay, as her doubts increased, the energy weakened.

As she watched, the intensity of the lightning faded. The creature found its balance again and brought its head forward to look right back at her with its beady red eyes. The monster was fighting back, recovering from the effects.

As those beast-like eyes focused on her and bored into her soul, it took a menacing step forward. Fear and anger flooded right back in as she let the doubts slip away. She would not die today.

"No!" she yelled.

Summoning up all her strength once more, Amanda dug deep, finding reservoirs of anger and frustration and she threw it all at the beast.

The energy more than doubled in ferocity, and with a final scream of unadulterated rage, Amanda let loose entirely.

With an ear-rattling boom, the creature was blasted against the wall with a final, powerful flare of lightning. As her last reserves of anger rushed out of her body and the energy faded away, she found herself alone in the alley.

The creature was gone, obliterated, and only a vaguely humanoid scorch mark on the wall remained.

Having risen to her knees for that final push, Amanda sat back down, nearly collapsing from the strain of what she'd just done. After taking a few moments to catch her breath, she looked at her hands as the last spluttering vestiges of energy sparked between her fingers and then disappeared.

What the hell had just happened? she wondered, as she turned her hands over, inspecting them for marks or burns. But there were none.

Looking around, the last few bits of burnt and blackened paper rippled to the ground, as the last vestiges of the golden mist that hung in the air faded from view.

Had she been attacked by a monster or a demon? But such things shouldn't exist. They were impossible. Monsters weren't real. Dragons and Vampires were myth and legend. It was one of those truths you learnt as a child along with there being no Easter Bunny or Santa Claus. There were no such things as werewolves or zombies. They were old myths, stories, and not real. And yet, here she was, sitting on the wet concrete of a Manhattan alley, cold and damp, having just been attacked by one. But not only that, she'd somehow thrown lightning bolts at it and killed it.

The world had gone mad, she thought as her eyes drifted over to the pile of bricks and rubble beneath which Stuart was buried. As she looked, she spotted a foot and a hand sticking out of the debris. She recognised the pristine white sneakers that Stuart had been wearing.

Amanda's heart sank. There was little trace of the Magic or the beast, but the aftermath of the confrontation was all too real.

Picking herself up out of the puddle, Amanda stood, the cold water dripping from her as she stepped over to the remains of her protector and friend. She went to reach for his hand but pulled back before she touched it. She couldn't bring herself to take it in hers.

"I'm sorry," she whispered to him. "You didn't deserve to die like this."

As she stood there, the sound of police sirens rose up from the background noise until Amanda suddenly registered their approach.

"Ah, crap."

***

The figure stood on top of the apartment block in the shadows of the building's water tank. She watched Amanda in the alley below, wobbling like a new-born fawn on her high heels, before she turned and ran as the sirens of the approaching police wailed.

The figure smiled. Finally, the moment she had been waiting on for all these centuries had come. Amanda had been through her Epiphany. But now, the real fun began. The next few years would be tough, and there was always a chance that things could go horribly wrong. The plans had been put in place, though, and everyone was ready to play their part.

Amanda had run out of sight now, so the figure stepped back, concentrated, and with a rush of Magical energy, disappeared.

- Internal missive within the Disciples of the Cross.

To: Grand Inquisitor Mary Damask
From: Grand High Inquisitor Valerio Rossi
Subject: Demon Sighting in New York

Inquisitor Damask,

I believe you have a man in New York currently?

We have had a credible sighting of a demon in Manhattan and a description of the witch who summoned it.

Notify your asset we will be monitoring the area. He needs to be ready to move as quickly as possible.

Please see the attachment for details and a description of the witch.

Updates to follow.
V.R.

The Inquisitor

JFK Airport

Amanda picked up her bag from the table and smiled meekly at the security guard who was standing on the other side, watching her.

"Thanks," she said.

The man nodded and turned to look at the other travellers behind her. Placing her roller bag on the floor and extending the handle, she walked away from the security checkpoint with a long, slow exhale. She concentrated on her breathing and did her best to calm herself down as she moved into the departure lounge.

Getting through check-in and security with her fake passport had been her biggest fear. Everything had gone through just fine, but she'd been terrified that she would get arrested at some point as she moved through the airport. Standing at that check-in desk, asking for an earlier flight as they scanned her passport, had been a moment of pure terror.

What if they'd found out she was living here illegally? She'd be deported eventually, sure, but that could take months, and Georgina had weeks or less to live.

She'd kept herself under control, though, and stood there smiling at the attendant as if this was the most normal thing in the world for her.

"Thank you, uh, Ms White," the attendant had said as she'd passed her documents back to her. She had no idea why the forger had used Alice White on the passport, but Amanda liked it.

Luckily, they'd found her a seat on an earlier flight, and she would be boarding her plane within the hour.

When the lady at the desk had said she could go through security into the departure lounge, part of her had been convinced it was part of some kind of elaborate trap. That the security teams were waiting for her and would detain her as she passed through, but there had been no problems at all. Her bag had been scanned, she'd walked through the metal detector, and everyone had treated her just like any other passenger.

A short walk later, Amanda sat herself down in one of the seats scattered around the departure lounge and did her best to relax. It wasn't that easy, however, and even though the worst part—and frankly, the riskiest part—was over, she found herself watching the airport security guards like a hawk. Keeping an eye out for any hint that they might be heading her way because her passport had been flagged somewhere.

So far, no one had approached her, and as the minutes passed, she started to breathe a little easier.

Looking around, she spotted a man sitting opposite her who was peering at her over his paper. He saw her notice him and looked away, focusing back on the newspaper he was reading. He was sat with a woman who was reading a novel.

Was he eyeing her up because she had a short, black and white tartan skirt on that showed off her legs? Or was he an undercover security guard getting info on her through a hidden earpiece? She started to feel nervous again and looked around at the other people in the lounge. A couple more people met her gaze, and suddenly she was feeling very uncomfortable. She felt sure it was merely coincidence and that she wasn't being watched, but her mind just wouldn't let the idea go.

She looked back at the man opposite her as she shifted her position and crossed her legs the other way. He was looking at her again, staring at her legs as she moved them.

He was probably just being a typical man, but the worry wouldn't slip away just yet.

The lady sitting next to the man looked up at him, followed his gaze, and looked at Amanda. She looked back at the woman, but she'd seen Amanda looking at her travelling companion. The woman turned to the man, who looked up from Amanda's legs and back at the woman. She rolled her eyes in exasperation. "Grow up, you perv. How old are you?" she muttered as the man went back to his paper, his cheeks burning scarlet.

Amanda smiled to herself. He was just admiring her, it seemed.

She'd been attacked only hours ago and every time she closed her eyes, her mind went straight back to that alleyway and the beast. Looking back at it now, surrounded by ordinary people in a busy airport, she wondered if it had all been a dream, or, more accurately, a nightmare.

Monsters didn't exist, and people couldn't throw lightning around, so what the hell had happened? Was she having a psychotic break? Was she hallucinating? Was Stuart actually dead?

Amanda's lips quivered and her eyes flooded as that thought hit her and then was quickly followed up with the thought that Georgina might not be long for this world either. Forcing herself to breathe, she pushed those emotions back down and blinked away her tears. She didn't want to start crying at the airport. She didn't want a fuss. She just wanted to get on the plane and go see her friend.

That's all that mattered. She'd think about the attack later. But not now.

A short time later, Amanda checked the departure board and spotted that the gate number had appeared next to her flight.

She stood and glanced at the couple sitting across from her again. The man looked up, his eyes drawn to her movements. Amanda smiled and winked at him. The man flushed and quickly looked back down at something in his paper that had suddenly become terribly interesting. Amanda walked away, smiling to herself, enjoying the moment.

Walking through the departure lounge to the gate, she felt relieved that she'd soon be in the air and away from the city. She'd always been a dreamer with an overactive imagination, which was usually a great thing to have, but there were times like this when she only saw threats around every corner. As usual, though, she'd imagined it and what she'd thought was an undercover agent was actually just a frustrated man who was enjoying the view.

She'd had plenty of experience with frustrated married men during her time on the streets of New York. They weren't getting what they desired from their relationship at home, so they came out to find it with people like Amanda and her friends. It always amused her when they tried to hide their wedding rings. She couldn't care less if they were married. She, like any working girl, was only interested in the contents of their wallet.

"Amanda?" said a male voice just behind her.

Turning, she looked at the man who'd said her name. He was tall with swarthy skin and a wiry frame. He looked like he'd lived his life out in the world and although his face was weathered, Amanda guessed he was probably in his thirties somewhere.

"Yes?" Amanda said, without really thinking about it.

The man smiled. "Excellent, would you come with me, please?"

Amanda frowned with consternation, wondering if she should have lied. He wasn't dressed in an airport uniform. Instead, he wore relatively dull, boring trousers, a dress shirt, and a long raincoat over the top. Was he a detective or something? she wondered.

"Who are you?" Amanda asked.

"I'm with airport security. If you'd like to follow me, please?" he said, moving to her side and putting his hand to the small of her back, urging her back the way she'd come.

"What's this about?" Amanda asked, resisting his attempts to move her.

"We just need to run some additional security checks, ma'am, it's nothing serious. You'll be on your way soon enough," he said.

Amanda narrowed her eyes at him. Something about this felt off. Even though she'd thought this might happen, convinced almost, something about this man didn't seem right. He had a strong Italian accent and wore a gold cross around his neck. Despite her doubts, Amanda started to walk in the direction he was guiding her. She could see a doorway up ahead that said *Staff Only* on it and guessed that must be where they were heading.

"What security checks? Did I fail something?" Amanda asked, trying to figure out what was going on.

"We'll talk more soon. I'm sure it's nothing to be worried about," he said, brushing off her concerns.

Amanda frowned again. This whole thing seemed wrong. They soon reached the door and the man pulled out a key. He unlocked it easily enough and directed Amanda through to the other side. The man followed her, shutting the door behind them.

"This way," the man said.

A man in an airport uniform was approaching them from the other direction. Was this one here for her as well? Amanda wondered. Glancing sideways as they set off up the hallway, she noticed that her captor was taking pains not to look at the approaching man, and in fact, seemed to be trying to hide his face, if anything.

The airport worker was frowning at them and watched closely as they passed each other. Two steps beyond the worker, Amanda heard him speak up.

"Hey, what are you doing back here?" he asked.

"Just dealing with a security issue," her captor said without stopping or looking back.

Amanda glanced back, though and saw the man frown at them as they continued walking.

"But security isn't that way," the man said.

This really wasn't right, Amanda thought. Something was very wrong here, so she slowed down and looked up at her captor. "What's your name?" Amanda asked. "Who do you work for? Where are you taking me?"

The man stopped too and looked at her through narrowed eyes that flashed with annoyance and possibly anger.

"Fine," the man said and reached into his inside coat pocket. She hadn't thought to ask for I.D. while they were in public, which was bloody stupid, she thought. That should have been the first thing she should have asked for back when there were way more people about.

The man withdrew his hand from his coat, but he wasn't holding identification. Instead, he pulled out a handgun with a very long barrel on it. Amanda had never shot a gun in her life, even during her time in America. She just didn't like them and had no idea what type of firearm it was. Her captor aimed the weapon at the worker and fired a single shot.

"No!" Amanda yelled.

She braced herself for a loud bang, but instead, the noise was more of a dull mechanical sound and surprisingly quiet. Amanda realised that the long barrel on the handgun was a silencer. For a moment, she wondered why they were called silencers when the gun wasn't actually silent. It was quieter than usual, for sure, but not silent.

The worker dropped to the floor. Amanda felt rooted to the spot and could only stare at the worker as he gasped for breath for a few seconds before falling still. She raised a hand to her mouth as realisation dawned.

"You... You shot him!" she stammered.

Her captor grabbed her by the arm and marched her over to a side door labelled *maintenance*. He had a face like thunder and seemed more than a little annoyed. He opened the door and looked inside. It was dark in the small room. Backing up, the man pointed the gun at Amanda. She sucked in a breath and raised her hands.

"Put him in there," he said.

"What?" Amanda asked, not really registering what the man had said to her.

"That guy, drag him into the closet. Now," he demanded.

Amanda looked at her captor's gun, and then at him. He'd shot the airport worker, so he might shoot her as well. She had no choice. She kicked off her high heels and walked up to the man's body. She'd never seen a dead body before and as she approached, she felt a little sick. Without realising it, she slowed down, delaying the moment that she'd have to touch him.

"Hurry up," the Italian man ordered her.

With a gulp, she stepped up to the body and reached down, grabbing his wrists. He was a lot heavier than he looked, but she put all her weight behind it and pulled, dragging him slowly towards the door of the maintenance closet, leaving a small trail of blood in their wake. Once inside the closet, Amanda let go of the body's wrists and took a moment to catch her breath. She felt shattered, but now she knew the truth. This man was not a part of airport security. In fact, she had no idea who he was or what he wanted with her.

This was all very strange, but then, her barometer for what was or wasn't strange had shifted somewhat recently.

What she did know for sure now, though, was that she needed to get away from this man as quickly as she could. He was dangerous, and she was likely to end up dead if she wasn't careful.

She frowned as she realised that right at that moment, the man was nowhere to be seen. Thinking she might have an opportunity here, Amanda padded silently over to the door, stepping over the corpse as she went, and tucked herself in beside the door. She glanced down at the body again, feeling suddenly very sorry for this man and his family. But now wasn't the time to get emotional, so she looked away and suppressed those emotions.

Amanda balled her fists as she waited and listened.

She heard footsteps approaching the door. He sighed and didn't sound too happy about something—probably how long it was taking her.

"Amanda," he said walking up to the door. "When you've finished in th…" he began as he stepped into the doorway. The second he appeared and hesitated upon seeing what looked like an empty room, Amanda stepped out and punched him hard in the face.

Her years on the street had taught her something about how to fight, and she knew how to throw a solid punch. She just hoped it was enough.

The man dropped his gun with a metallic clatter as Amanda stepped around the corner. He took the blow well, though, and immediately went for her. This clearly wasn't his first time getting hit. Amanda moved back, stepping nimbly over the body, but the man had forgotten about it and caught his foot on the corpse. Her captor staggered into the room and fell to his knees.

Amanda rushed over to him and channelled all her rage into her fist as she wound it back. She might not know this man's name, but she knew enough to know she didn't like him. She swung her fist and smashed him in his face, noticing a crackle of blue and golden energy around her hand that had not been there a heartbeat ago.

As her punch connected, the energy in her fist appeared to jump between them and wash over the man before fading away.

Amanda jumped back in surprise. "What the feck?" she muttered to herself as the man dropped to the floor, his eyes rolling back into his skull. She'd seen this curious golden energy before, but this was the first time she's seen it on or around herself.

Feeling flustered, she wanted to run but forced herself to check on the man she'd just hit. He was unconscious. With a brief nod, Amanda stepped out of the room and pulled the door shut behind her. Hopping over to her shoes, she slipped them back on and regarded the bloodstain on the floor. It was a small smear, and it appeared that the Italian had made an attempt to clean it up a bit while she'd been moving the body.

Amanda paused. Should she tell someone? Should she inform security? As she stood there thinking what to do, she heard the voice on the loudspeaker announce the last call for her flight to Ireland. Although she felt terrible for doing it, she made her choice. She headed back the way she'd come, back out into the busy terminal, and jogged up to her gate. She needed to get to Ireland. Someone else could clear up this mess. Anyway, the Italian was only unconscious and would likely wake up at some point soon. She didn't want to be here when that happened.

- Manhattan, New York

Vito stood on the New York street and rubbed his face. It was still sore after that bitch had punched him in the airport. He felt incredibly frustrated by that whole affair. He'd nearly had her, but now he felt like an idiot. He hadn't checked where she was flying to or what the name on her—no doubt fake—passport was, so he had no way of finding her that way.

So, here he was, in the middle of New York surrounded by more infuriating Yanks, watching the girls who, according to their eyewitness, had been working the streets with Amanda. He wasn't sure which of them were Amanda's friends, but he would find out, and he would make them talk.

He was looking forward to finishing this mission as soon as possible and getting back to Rome. He despised the USA with its garish, ungodly culture. The sooner he was back in the Vatican, the better.

Still, there was always a silver lining in every cloud, and today's would be the enjoyment of getting these girls to tell him what he needed to know. The fact that his targets were not only prostitutes, but also American ones, just made the idea even sweeter.

If this Amanda-witch had any sense about her, she wouldn't have left a forwarding address with any of her former heretic friends after her summoning of the demon in the alleyway. But, you never knew your luck, and it would be fun finding out.

He'd also pay a visit to the alleyway to see if there were any clues there, too. Maybe the grace of God would reveal something useful to him.

A chance meeting

Donegal, Ireland

It was early July and the sun was shining through the windows of the cottage with an inviting, golden glow. She'd take a walk shortly and get some fresh air, but for now, she was just enjoying her mug of hot chocolate. She wanted to focus on the little things, the small joys in life and try to forget some of her other, larger problems.

Not that they were problems or even concerns any more. The only issue now was, how she would move on with her life. What she'd do next. But that was a question she didn't have an answer for.

When she'd arrived here over a month ago, she'd found Georgina in a much worse state than she'd expected. She was a shadow of her former self and completely bedridden by then. Amanda could see that she was fading fast and wouldn't be alive for much longer.

Days later, she passed away. It was almost as if she'd been waiting for Amanda to come to her bedside. Georgina had told her how happy she was to have Amanda there and away from the streets. She made Amanda promise never to work the streets again, ever.

She had the sense that Georgina felt guilty that Amanda had ended up as a working girl, but Amanda had reassured her that it was her choice and not Georgina's. She probably would have ended up doing it anyway, or something similar, or worse. Besides, she was alive, she'd survived, and she was never going back.

Georgina asked after Stuart and the others. Amanda had lied. She couldn't face telling her that Stuart was dead, nor could she bring herself to tell Georgina about the strange encounters she'd experienced. It was just more stress that Georgina didn't need. Amanda spent her time trying to keep Georgina's spirits up and helping the nurses who visited to care for her now that she was in the final stage of her life. There was nothing that could be done. Her body was shutting down. She would die, no matter what.

The money Georgina had gained from the inheritance paid for everything, including this cottage and her care. She was as comfortable as she could be, and Georgina had already put the remainder into Amanda's name. Amanda could live here for as long as she wanted and never need to worry about money.

Amanda had never found out who this long-lost family member was who had given Georgina the cottage and the money. But then, Georgina hadn't seemed to know who it was, either. It was something of a coincidence that the cottage was here, in Donegal, just a few miles away from where Amanda had grown up in the orphanage, but life was full of coincidences that only gave you a headache if you thought about them for too long.

The cottage felt so quiet now, out here in the countryside of Ireland, with Georgina gone. She'd been rattling around in the house for a few weeks, trying to force herself to go out, to enjoy the countryside and the weather as much as possible.

The funeral had happened quickly and only Amanda and the nurses attended. Georgina had been cremated, as per her request. That had been a sad day. Amanda had come back to the cottage that night and cried herself to asleep. In fact, it was only in recent days that she'd started to get through a whole day without shedding a single tear.

Taking a breath, she tried her best to push those thoughts to the back of her mind. This was her birthday, and she didn't want to spend the day moping about. Georgina wouldn't want that. She'd want her to have a happy day.

She felt like she'd been upset ever since she'd arrived here, but it wasn't doing her any good, and her friend certainly wouldn't want her to feel this way each and every day.

Here she was, back in Ireland, her home country, with more money than she knew how to spend, but she had no clue what she wanted to do with her life and therein lies the problem.

Something she'd started to do each day was to exercise. It felt good, allowed her time to think, and was infinitely better than being alone in the cottage day after day. She'd taken to going for a run every day and exploring the local countryside. On one such trip, she'd found a picturesque clearing in the forest. There was something almost magical about the place. It felt like the kind of place fairies might gather, or was that her overactive imagination again?

She didn't care, all she knew was that she liked it and in this weather, it was the perfect sunbathing spot.

After she'd finished her drink, she got herself up properly, pulling on her running clothes—which in this warm weather, was only a sports bra and lycra shorts with socks and running shoes—before she stepped outside.

It was mid-morning and the sun was streaming into the valley. The cottage was close to the Blue Stack Mountains in Donegal at the bottom of a wide depression with hills on three sides. From her front door, she couldn't even see the next closest house. A single muddy track led out of the valley with her cottage at the end of it. Beyond that, a little way up the valley, was the forest that Amanda enjoyed exploring. But before she went there, she set off on her run. She took a wide arc around the valley, running up and down the slopes, pumping her legs and feeling the burn as she jogged. Her whitewashed cottage was an idyllic looking place. L-shaped, with a thatched roof and a modest garden surrounded by a picket fence. She found it hard to believe that this was hers now, but she had the documents to prove it. She owned it. This was her home.

Close to an hour later, as the sun climbed to its highest point, Amanda made her way to the edge of the woods and slowed to a walk before heading inside. She loved walking in here, making her way through the long grass with the dappled sunlight playing over the landscape, lighting up parts of the woods while leaving other areas in the shade. The birds sang from the tree tops and she could hear the movement of wildlife in the undergrowth, always just out of sight.

Soon enough, she found her clearing again and stepped out from the treeline. Just inside the clearing was an old tree stump, so Amanda made her way over there and sat down. Her muscles ached, but it was a good feeling. She knew she'd worked hard and pushed herself. She closed her eyes and concentrated on slowing her breathing, forcing herself to relax.

She pulled the air in through her nose and out through her mouth, moving the life-giving oxygen through her body, slowly and methodically.

As she sat there, feeling relaxed and calm, her cares floating away on the light breeze that caressed her skin and pulled at the strands of her hair, she started to feel tingling around her head and neck. She got it occasionally when she was relaxed, and when she'd looked into it she found it was called Autonomous Sensory Meridian Response, or ASMR for short. It was a feeling only some people experienced when they were in a state of relaxation and it could be brought on by lots of different stimuli.

Amanda had felt it before when she'd been in Howie's arms watching a film, and he'd been playing with her hair, or when she'd had someone be particularly gentle with her when doing her hair or makeup. It wasn't in the slightest bit sexual—quite the opposite. It was calming and relaxing and made her want to fall asleep.

Opening her eyes, Amanda could make out a strange glowing golden mist, rising up from the ground and hanging in the air.

She could still see the world around her, it didn't obscure anything at all, but it was there, as real as the tree stump she sat on.

She'd seen it a few times recently, but never when she'd expected to. She had no idea what it was. The first few times she'd experienced it she'd been shocked and recoiled from the vision, but she knew it wasn't anything to worry about now, so she calmly accepted it. She hoped she'd find out what it was soon, though.

Feeling totally relaxed, Amanda stepped off the tree stump and sat herself down in the grass, pulled off her trainers and socks, and then her sports bra and shorts so she could sunbathe in only her underwear. She didn't like tan lines, and she'd never seen anyone come up here, so she wasn't worried about anyone seeing her topless.

She laid in the grass and enjoyed the feeling of the sun's heat on her skin. She turned every so often, but she must have nodded off because she suddenly woke up, positive that she'd just heard something. Propping herself up, she spotted someone else in the clearing.

It was a man, over towards the middle, quite a distance away from her.

At first, she was offended. She felt like this was her clearing, her secret place, but she knew that was ridiculous. This was a public space; anyone could come here. The man was going about his business and seemed to be either ignoring her, or he was unaware that she was even there. What was he doing? she thought. But then, after a few seconds, it was obvious. He was doing Tai Chi or something similar.

As she watched, the shock of seeing someone else here faded away to be replaced with a kind of fascination. The man looked to be in his fifties and was of Chinese descent, if she had to guess. His movements were calm and precise as he slowly worked through his routine, reaching and stretching. It was incredibly graceful and utterly fascinating.

After a while, as she relaxed, she could feel the tingles around her forehead and temples grow again. She ended up just sitting there, watching and enjoying the show as the tingles moved through her hair and over her neck. She wasn't sure how long it went on for and she didn't care, but after a while he stopped. She was so chilled out, it took Amanda a few moments to realise that his routine was over. She watched as he picked up a towel from the grass and walked off towards the far edge of the clearing.

As he went he glanced back once, looking right at her, before continuing on his way.

Amanda half-smiled at him as he looked, before suddenly realising she was still topless. She laughed to herself. She'd probably scared him off. She lay back down a little while longer before pulling clothes back on and making her way back home, feeling completely relaxed and calm.

Before she'd left the cottage this morning, she'd found it tough to think of anything other than Georgina and she'd found herself thinking that the cottage kind of represented her death. There was almost a miasma of sadness about the place.

But on her return, that had gone. Now, she looked at the small white building with its thatched roof and saw something that was hers. She saw her home. A place she could live in and enjoy. There were some sad memories attached to it still, but they no longer dominated it. They were there should she need to remember her friend, but there were new feelings associated with it now, the main ones being hope and love.

The Chinese man had fascinated Amanda, and she wondered if he would be there again the next day. So, she returned and waited, and sure enough, he came back and went through his routine once more.

This time, Amanda sat on the tree stump to get a better look. Again the man's slow, measured movement served to relax her so she could feel those pleasant tingles, but this time, she also saw the golden mist. But what was curious and wondrous was that as the man moved, he seemed to interact with the mist, and there were times when she felt sure that the man himself appeared infused with it and glowed slightly.

As he left that day, he looked back at Amanda again and actually smiled at her. His face was friendly and kind.

Later on that night, as she sat before her open fire, she decided she'd go and speak to him the next time she saw him. She didn't want to scare him off by being there every day and watching him like some kind of silent stalker. It seemed only right that she introduce herself and say hello.

The man returned again on the third day, and after watching him run through his routine, Amanda got up and walked over as he wiped his brow with his towel. The man was short, easily under five feet tall, and it seemed odd to be looking down at a grown adult to talk to him. She was usually the one looking up. He was quite a handsome man with his bald head, moustache, and small beard at the end of his chin. He looked up at her as she approached.

"Heh, Hi," she said. "How are yeh?"

He smiled. "I am well, thank you," he said in heavily Chinese accented English.

"So, um, I hope you don't mind me asking, but was that Tai Chi you were doing?" she asked, feeling much more nervous than she thought she would.

He smiled. "I see why you think that it Tai Chi," he said with his pleasing accent. "But no, it not Tai Chi. I practice Art of Phoenix."

Amanda liked him right away. His voice had a calming quality to it, and she found the way he left out words—probably because English wasn't his first language, she guessed—rather cute.

"The Art of the Phoenix? That's grand, I've not heard of that before," she said.

"It from Tibet, deep in mountains. I learn it from my master, Graceful Phoenix at Red Monastery."

"Well, it's beautiful to watch, so it is."

The man bowed slightly with a smile.

"I hope you don't mind me watching you," Amanda added.

"No. I don't mind," he said.

"So, have you been coming to this clearing for long?" she asked, wondering if she'd missed him during her previous visits before seeing him the other day.

"No, not long. But it very relaxing, yes?"

"Very," Amanda smiled.

"You know Tai Chi?" he asked.

Amanda smiled. "I don't. I've learnt a little self-defence in my time, so I have, but not Tai Chi."

"You want learn?"

"Maybe, one day," she said.

"Tomorrow?"

"Sorry, what?"

"You learn Art of Phoenix with me tomorrow. Yes?"

"You're offering to teach me?" Amanda asked, incredulous. She couldn't quite believe that he was asking her if she wanted to learn from him.

"Yes," he said, nodding with a smile.

"Well, I…" Amanda hesitated.

"You say yes. You learn from me."

"Okay, well, sure, why not?" Amanda said, not wanting to disappoint him.

"Excellent," the man answered.

"Oh, um, I'm Amanda, by the way. Amanda-Jane Page," she said, offering her hand.

The man took her hand in his and bowed to her. "I am Gentle Water."

Amanda cocked her head slightly to one side and couldn't help the brief frown that crossed her face. "That's an... unusual name," she said, hoping she didn't offend him with her choice of words.

"Yes. It not my birth name, but it my name from Red Monastery. I like."

Amanda nodded. She liked it too and thought it suited him well. She could already tell that he was a calm and methodical man. She liked him.

"I see you tomorrow at same time?" he asked.

"Of course." She smiled and said goodbye to him. She watched him walk off before turning and setting off back to her side of the clearing and the cottage.

She couldn't help the smile that played over her face as she walked. For the first time since she'd returned to Ireland, she not only felt hope for the future, but she felt like she had some kind of direction. Meeting Gentle Water had come at just the right moment and she was looking forward to seeing him again tomorrow and maybe becoming his student.

Meeting him like that reminded her of meeting Alicia, her childhood friend from her days in the orphanage.

She'd never known her parents, having been found as a baby on the doorstep of an orphanage and convent school, not too far from where she lived now. She'd been taken in by the nuns there and named Amanda-Jane, after the two sisters who found her and given the surname of Page, which was the surname of the Mother Superior, Emmanuelle Page. She'd grown up within the walls of the orphanage, raised by the nuns, but she'd always been something of a free spirit and a little wild. As she grew up, it only got worse, though. She was forever getting into trouble for disobeying the nuns. Their punishments could be harsh, but Amanda didn't care. In fact, it only drove her to do worse or more daring stuff. Looking back now at the child she'd been, she saw a young girl she didn't like very much. Someone who really should have known better, but at the time, she'd felt trapped in a cage. She'd spent her whole life in that place, and she longed for release.

She'd run away a couple of times, but the police had always found her and brought her back and yet, she was forever planning her next attempt.

Having lived there since she was a baby, Amanda knew the building very well, better than most of the nuns, and she'd found several places she could hide or sneak into to be by herself. One of them was a roof space that she could reach a couple of ways, the main one being up a disused chimney and through a hole partway up.

If the sisters knew of it, they'd have had it blocked up, so she'd kept it to herself.

She spent her time up there daydreaming about the places she'd visit one day when she could get out of the orphanage. The place she dreamt about most often was New York. She loved the look of the big city and collected photos of it that she pinned to the rafters up in her roof space.

She'd spent hours lying up there, staring at those images, imagining walking the streets and looking up at the towering skyscrapers.

Looking back, she wondered how her life would have gone had Alicia not joined the orphanage. She'd been on the road to self-destruction, she thought now, but Alicia had seen something in her. She'd seen that this delinquent red-headed girl was acting out and chose to take it upon herself to change things. She couldn't know for sure, of course, but Alicia must have had thoughts along those lines.

Alicia was a model student at the school. Diligent in her work, she followed the rules but was friendly and open. She was a popular girl and seemed to befriend anybody. Amanda disliked her from the moment they'd met and made a point of avoiding her, which was somewhat ironic, really.

Maybe she'd sensed that Alicia would rein her in and so she kept her distance. But once Alicia had made up her mind to befriend Amanda, there was no stopping her. No matter how horrible she was to Alicia, she always came back, and in the end, Amanda couldn't resist any longer.

The thing was though, that once she let her barriers down and let Alicia get close, she found that she actually really liked the girl. She was friendly, bubbly, and against everything that Amanda had previously thought, they quickly became very close friends.

The effect Alicia had on her was profound, and within weeks her grades were up, and she was no longer causing trouble. The wild side of Amanda was still there, of course, and despite the best efforts of the nuns and Alicia, who was a devout Catholic, Amanda was never interested in all that God stuff. She found it boring and tedious. She wanted to live, to enjoy life, and not spend it on her knees.

She did, however, respect Alicia for her unshakable faith. It clearly had a positive impact on her and her life. In turn, Alicia herself then had a positive effect on Amanda, and for that, she was eternally grateful.

When she did finally run away from the orphanage after the pressure of living there got too much for her, the one regret she had was leaving Alicia. She hadn't told anyone about her plans, not even Alicia. She didn't want to jeopardise her chances. Alicia probably had guessed where Amanda had gone, though, as she knew about her obsession with New York City. Amanda had shown her the roof space with all the photos she'd cut out of books and magazines, but only after Alicia had promised never to show or tell anyone else about it.

One day, she hoped to return to the orphanage to find out what had happened to her friend. But not yet. She wasn't ready yet.

- Diary entry of Royston Kendrick, Spokesperson for the Legacy Coven.

Gentle Water reported in today. He's made contact with Amanda in Ireland. Met her a few times over the last few days and is starting to teach her the basics of his martial arts style.

At least we can relax for a bit now. The meeting was always going to be touch and go, despite the reassurances of our friend.

I must keep in regular contact with him.

Revelation

Donegal, Ireland

The summer had turned out to be a rather nice one with plenty of warm weather, which made a nice change to the usual rain and clouds that Ireland was known for. Amanda lay in her bed, enjoying another lazy morning, watching the sunlight play through the gap in her curtains and create patterns on the wall. As she lay there, she heard the door to the cottage open and close.

It was Gentle Water, heading out as he usually did in the mornings. He wasn't one for lying in his bed. It had been nearly two months since she had first spoken to him in the clearing, which had become their primary practice area for the martial arts he was teaching her. They'd spent more time together as he taught her that the Art of the Phoenix was more than just a relaxation tool, it was a whole martial art that could be used as a weapon as well.

She'd soon found out that Gentle Water was staying in a hotel in the next town over, and after some thought and several weeks of training, Amanda decided to offer him the second bedroom in her cottage.

Apparently, Gentle Water had been travelling and liked the area, so he was staying locally to get a feel for the place before he found somewhere more permanent. But they were spending so much time together now, it seemed to her to just make sense that he live with her for a while.

Gentle Water was unsure at first, but eventually agreed to move into the cottage for the short-term, at least. As the weeks wore on, they became fast friends, with Gentle Water taking on something of a fatherly role for her. She'd never had a dad or a male role model in her life. All she'd had were the nuns and the girls in her dorm. There were boys at the convent school, but they only saw each other during lessons and breaks, so she'd always been somewhat starved of male role models.

She didn't regret the way things had been back then, but it was nice to have someone like that in her life now. Gentle Water remained somewhat aloof, however. He was quiet and kept to himself, generally staying out of Amanda's way as much as possible. She wondered if he felt that he was imposing on her, because she didn't feel that way at all. She'd invited him to live with her, and she actually really enjoyed having him around.

But she had a feeling that he was holding something back from her. Hiding something, but she had no idea what it could be.

Maybe he'd open up to her at some point, once he was ready. She didn't want to pry, everyone had secrets after all, and they'd only known each other for a few weeks. She felt she knew him well enough now, though, that she had no issues with him being in the house with her. He was kind, respectful, and very gentlemanly, always going out of his way to help her and do what needed doing around the house.

Amanda reached out for the glass of water by her bed and out the corner of her eye, saw it slide across the top of the bedside table and into her hand. She looked at it properly, squinting at it.

Had it really just done that?

It wasn't the first time. In fact, strange things had been happening to her for years. Things she couldn't explain, but were always subtle and often—like just now with the water glass—she'd catch it out of the corner of her eye so she was never sure if it had really happened or not.

However, since the attack in New York, the frequency of these oddities had changed dramatically. Before that day, they were sporadic, maybe two or three times a year, four or five occasionally, but they were always subtle, and she was never sure if she'd just imagined it.

Now, though, they were happening daily, often several times a day, and they seemed to be growing in frequency. Just last night, she'd seen the gold mist again and had moved a coffee mug to her hand, right next to Gentle Water. She was sure he must have seen it, but when she asked, he said he hadn't seen anything and brushed it off.

Sometimes they freaked her out, but they were becoming so common now that she'd actually started to accept them.

Sitting up, she took a gulp of her drink then got up and padded around to the bathroom. Pulling off her nightclothes, she jumped into the shower and enjoyed the soothing feeling of water hammering against her skin.

Getting used to Gentle Water being in the house had been interesting. She'd been so used to living alone both in her New York apartment and now here, that she would often walk about either nude or just in her underwear, such as from the shower. She'd only forgotten herself once and probably given Gentle Water something of an eyeful as she stepped out of the bathroom wearing nothing but a towel on her head. He'd been so quiet that morning that she'd forgotten he was living with her.

She apologised, of course, but he'd laughed it off.

Finishing up, she reached for the towel and once again felt sure that the thing had just leapt into her hand. Blinking the water out of her eyes, she frowned at it.

This was getting silly.

Exiting the shower, she dried herself and got dressed, pulling on a pair of cropped leggings and a sports top.

A drink, a slice of toast, and two more instances of objects moving on their own later, and she was out the door, jogging up the slope towards the tree line.

She soon made it through the woods to the clearing and wandered into the open space, spotting Gentle Water up ahead. As she walked towards him, something looked odd. His position on the ground looked a long way away and yet she knew he was closer than that. The perspective of the whole scene seemed off and wrong. She continued forward, and suddenly her brain made sense of what she was seeing. She stopped, frozen in place, struggling to fully comprehend what she was looking at.

Gentle Water was sitting cross-legged and floating several feet off the ground.

"What the feck?" she whispered.

Gentle Water opened his eyes and looked at her. He smiled a warm, friendly smile that softened her shock. "Don't be afraid. I explain everything," he said as he put his feet down and stood.

"What is going on?" she asked. "What are you?"

Gentle Water smiled. "*We* are Magi," he said, pronouncing the last word with a hard G so it sounded like *Ma-Guy*.

"We?" Amanda asked.

"That is right. You can use Magic. Real Magic. Not card tricks or stage magic, but real-life Magic."

"Feck off," Amanda said. "That's rubbish."

"I have seen you use it. I know you see things. I come here to find you, help you because you are Magi."

Again with that strange word, she thought. "Magic?"

"You know what I speak of. You can move things with your mind. You see things. Like glowing mist, yes?"

Amanda nodded. "Well, yeah, I suppose…"

"Magic," he said.

"It's just… I can't believe it. It's not possible. Magic can't be…"

"Real? But it is. Search inside your soul. Find truth. You know I right. I know what you have seen. I know about alley in New York. I know about attack there. You are Magi, Amanda. So am I. Let me show you."

There was a brief rush of air and a flash of light behind her eyelids as she felt something, some kind of energy surge within her. A simultaneous rush of dislocation and the feeling that up was down briefly made Amanda crouch, scared that she was about to tip over, but the sensation was gone just as quickly as it had appeared, and suddenly they were on top of one of the turrets of Edinburgh Castle.

"Holy shite!" Amanda cursed. She reached out and touched the stone of the castle to make sure it was real. "How did you…?"

There was another flash, another whip of wind and the feeling of dislocation, and they were stood atop the biggest pyramid at Giza in Egypt. The heat here was oppressive; it felt as if they'd just appeared in an oven. Amanda stumbled and fell to her knees, gripping the sandstone beneath her with her hands.

"This can't be real, this is crazy," she said.

"This is Magic, and you will do this, too, one day," Gentle Water said from where he stood next to her.

The energy surged once more, and they stood on the roof of the Freedom Tower in New York City.

"Okay, okay, I get it. It's real," Amanda said, feeling more than a little overwhelmed, not to mention nauseated. Gentle Water smiled again, and with another surge of energy, they were back in the clearing.

Kneeling on the ground, Amanda had never felt so pleased to be back in Ireland. She dropped to the ground entirely, resting her head against the dew-covered grass for a moment as the strange feeling of dizziness faded.

"Are you okay?" Gentle Water asked.

"Heh, yeah, I'm grand," she said as she stood back up, feeling slightly better. "Okay, so, Magic is real. Consider me convinced. What does that mean for me?"

"You are Magi," he answered her.

"Why do you keep saying it like that? I've heard the word before, but isn't it pronounced Meh-Jai?"

"The generic word, yes, but not when referring to us. We have own word for what we are, that word is said Mah-Guy," he answered her.

"Okay, grand. I understand that. But what does that mean? Are there lots of us? Who are these Magi?"

"The Magi have been around for thousands of years, Amanda. Hidden in shadows, fighting the darkness, protecting humanity. We are called Arcadians. We are global organisation. We protect Riven."

"Riven?"

"Humans with no Magic," he answered her. "We fight the Nomads. Nomads are dark Magi, evil Magi who serve ancient beings called Archons who live in Abyss, the Spirit world."

"Okay, so, two factions, the Arcadians and Nomads, and they're at war?"

"That is right, yes. There is also other group, younger group who fight all other Magi, only two thousand year old. They are Disciples of Cross or Inquisition."

"The Inquisition? As in the Catholic Inquisition?"

"Yes. They based in Vatican, led by Disciple Simon Peter."

"*The* Simon Peter, Jesus' disciple?" Amanda asked, shocked at the meaning of this revelation.

"Yes."

"But, he would be… Nearly two thousand years old…"

Gentle Water nodded at her, his eyes twinkling as he spoke. "He is young, we know Magi that are thousands of years older than him. Some Magi can live for very long time."

"So, Jesus was real? God is real?"

"We think he was just Magus who started cult. When you old enough to see religions and civilisations rise and fall, then you realise truth of world."

"Magus?"

"Singular version of Magi," he explained.

"Aaah," she said in understanding.

Amanda felt bewildered by what Gentle Water was telling her, but also fascinated. Having grown up in a Catholic convent school, she'd been taught bible studies throughout her childhood, and now she was being told they were not entirely accurate. She supposed, given the miracles that Jesus was supposed to have enacted, it would make a lot of sense if he'd been Magi.

"So, were all Jesus' disciples Magi? Were they like a group of Magi?"

"Perhaps. Magi often live in group. These groups called covens. Arcadians have council, too."

"Do the Nomads have one? Like, a council of evil?"

Gentle Water smiled. "No. Nomads don't work together well. They have covens, but not council," he said.

Gentle Water led her over to a rug on the ground nearby and sat down with her. Amanda thought over what he'd said. So, there were three factions of Magi—the Arcadians, the Nomads, and the Inquisition—and it sounded like they didn't really get on with each other. Thinking about her recent experiences, though, something didn't fit. She'd been attacked by something that was not human in New York. Surely, that wasn't a Magus. She looked up at Gentle Water and frowned as she thought about how to phrase the question. Then she remembered he said he knew of the attack in the alleyway, so she jumped right in.

"So, what attacked me in New York?" she asked.

"Aaah, that was Scion," he said. "Long time ago, thousands of years, when Archons still on Earth, they each create servants, a bloodline of creatures: transformed humans into monsters. Vampires, werewolves, and other beasts. All are real. Some still serve Archons or Nomads, but all are real. You were attacked by Horlack. He very old Scion. Lucky you go through Epiphany."

"Epiphany?" Amanda asked.

"Yes. Your Magical awakening, when you realise Magic is real and gain new understanding."

"You mean when I fired lightning at him? That was my Epiphany?"

"Yes. Epiphanies often take form of great Magic."

"Wow. That was lucky. So, if I was attacked by a Scion in the alleyway, I'm guessing that the man in the airport was an Inquisitor, given the cross he was wearing at the time," she thought out loud to herself. She noticed Gentle Water nod as she spoke. "This is a lot to take in."

"I know. Sorry."

"No, no, that's fine. I'll think it through later. So, I can use Magic?"

"Yes. Magic is powered by Essentia, Magical Energy, which you see as glowing mist. You are already strong in Magic, Amanda, you just need to accept it and learn to use it. I teach you."

"That would be awesome." Amanda smiled back at him in unrestrained glee. "So, what kind of stuff can I do?"

"All kind of things. You can make things appear, travel great distance in blink of eye, throw fire and lightning, and heal any wound or illness. Almost anything possible, Amanda," he explained.

"Anything is possible," she repeated in wonderment. "I just... I still need to get my head around this.". It sounded like she'd been subconsciously using magic for a while, until her Epiphany when she was finally able to use it for real and kill that Scion.

Amanda made a sudden connection in her mind and her giddy smile began to fade as a realisation dawned. She looked up at Gentle Water.

"So, I could use Magic from the moment of my Epiphany?"

"Correct, young one."

"And, Magic can heal people?"

"That is true."

"Ah shite," Amanda said as she thought about Georgina and the possibility that she could have saved her. Had she realised it, had she pursued it and tried to harness the power within her, maybe Georgina would still be here.

"What is wrong?" Gentle Water asked.

"I could have saved her," she muttered. "If I'd known, if I'd realised, maybe I could have done something." She'd decided to put her experience in the alleyway to one side when she got to Ireland. She'd chosen not to tell Georgina and to instead just be there for her. She'd been passive rather than active. She could have done something but didn't, and now her friend was dead.

"Amanda. You not know then. You not understand Magic. You must not blame self," her mentor said. And yet, she couldn't help it. She could have saved her, she'd had that chance, but now that chance was gone and so was her friend.

"But I could have."

"Then learn from it. Take your pain. Hold it close and learn from it."

- Grand Inquisitor Marcus' report on Horlack's Disappearance. July 1204 AD.

It seems my old enemy, my nemesis, has disappeared. I tracked him and his forces to Constantinople, but it seems that he vanished during the chaos of that glorious siege. I don't believe that my old foe has been killed. I feel it in my bones that he's still alive, somewhere.

I shall not rest until he is found, by the honour of the Disciples of the Cross, I swear this with God as my witness.

Acquisition

Cairo, Egypt

Wandering through the Markets in Cairo, Stephen could not be happier. The place was amazing. It was filled with hundreds of stalls selling all kinds of weird and wonderful stuff. Everything from beautiful carpets and clothing, to spices and foods—many of which he'd never seen before. The air was filled with rich aromas that assaulted his senses, and every turn revealed a new scent.

He was here with his parents, and it was funny to watch the locals spot them and try to sell them something. They stood out from the crowd with their western clothes and pale skin. A couple of people had already attempted to buy his mother. He had no idea if they were serious or if they were just having fun, playing up to the stereotypes which they surely knew about.

Cairo was a curious mix of old and new. One moment, they were looking at a wood-framed stall selling brightly-coloured spices from terracotta pots, a scene that had probably remained unchanged for hundreds of years, and then the stallholder would pull out their ringing mobile phone, or Stephen would spot a fast-food restaurant in the background.

The mix of cultures was fascinating.

As they wandered, Stephen looked for some kind of souvenir to take home. Something he could show his friends. Something that would fit their interests.

Stephen's father worked for the Natural History Museum in London, and he was always bringing strange new artifacts home or photos of the museum's latest acquisition. Having been surrounded by mystical artifacts his whole life, Stephen had grown up with a fascination of myth, legend, and magic. He was convinced that there was something to these stories from around the world, that there was an element of truth in there, and after that séance he'd had with his three friends the other week, he'd become even more sure of it.

He wished he could have brought Ben, Francesca, and Liz with him; they would have loved it here. Especially the girls, who were more into the occult than even he was.

Their friendship grew from a couple of chance encounters and was based on a mutual interest in Science Fiction, Fantasy, and the occult. Ben, a local kid who lived in a council estate not too far from Stephen, had caught him reading a comic. Ben was a huge comic book geek—something he kept hidden from his mates on the estate—and he seemed relieved to find someone he could share his interest with. They practically never mixed while in school as their friendship circles were just too different, but outside of school, they were close friends.

His friendship with Fran and her sister Liz came about sometime after befriending Ben, when he'd been forced to partner up with Fran during a science class. He'd been daydreaming during one of the lessons and had been doodling in his notebook, sketching out pentagrams and stuff. Francesca noticed them and started to ask questions. It turned out that the girl he'd considered to be a bit odd and not someone he was interested in was also into myths and legends. He remembered her looking at his sketches and calling them cool. Her comment, and the way she looked at him in that moment, changed the way he viewed her. When he'd first met up with Fran and Ben outside of school, she'd brought her sister, Liz along with her, too. They were identical twins, but could not have been more different in appearance.

Fran had dyed her hair copper and wore it in loose waves that fell over her shoulders. That night, she also wore a short, ripped denim skirt over a pair of leggings and several layers of old tops beneath a denim jacket that had seen better days. She walked confidently in her high heels and greeted them warmly.

By comparison, Liz was dressed in a warm high-necked sweater, long coat, jeans, and sneakers, and wore her long blonde hair loose and straight.

It was only in their faces that you could see any resemblance between them.

They'd met up regularly ever since and were good friends. As they talked more about their interests, he remembered Fran saying that she and Liz could sometimes make things move with their minds, like some kind of telekinesis. He and Ben had laughed at the idea, of course, but didn't dismiss it, and when the opportunity presented itself, they set up some candles and tried to mimic the séance-like situation that the girls had been in when this phenomenon had first happened.

When that first candle had risen up and floated before them, suddenly the idea of magic or psychic powers didn't seem quite so far-fetched, or quite so funny.

They'd repeated the exercise several times on different days, and Fran said that she and Liz were practising their ability whenever they could. More recently, the girls moved heavier items and had scared Ben and Stephen with their talent, such as when he'd pissed Fran off, and she'd unconsciously moved a nearby car as she'd shouted at him. Stephen was of the private opinion that the girls weren't fully aware of the extent of their powers and were more powerful than they knew. Whatever the case, woe betide anyone who really made them angry because they'd probably end up as a stain on the wall.

The girls were convinced it was some kind of magic. Ben, on the other hand, thought it was some kind of psychic ability. Stephen wasn't sure what it was, but he felt there must be an explanation for it.

They were always looking for mystical books and any resources they could find. They had taken to visiting a couple of magic shops in London that carried strange and curious items, hoping to find something useful.

When he'd told his friends he was visiting Egypt, he promised them he'd be on the lookout for anything strange and he'd been looking forward to exploring the markets to see what he could find. He'd heard tales of tomb robbers selling their wares through markets like this one and hoped to find something of interest.

He'd found a few stalls already that were selling so-called artifacts, but nothing really leapt out at him or looked authentic.

Spotting another stall covered with more trinkets, he stepped over to it, his parents just behind him, and started to look over the items for sale.

He spotted the usual miniature pyramids, busts of Nefertiti, Tutankhamun's mask, and statues of the gods of ancient Egypt, but again, nothing of great interest.

Stephen sighed, smiled at the vendor and turned away.

"You not find anything you like?" the vendor called after him.

"No, sorry," Stephen said, looking back.

"I have more. Come, come round, you see," he said, waving Stephen around the side of the stall. He glanced at his parents, who smiled and watched, urging him to go and have a look.

Feeling more confident, he moved around to where the trader sat behind the stall. He had a small table set out with a range of items on it, from tiny bits of jewellery to a huge stone slab that was covered in detailed carvings.

This last item caught Stephen's eye, and he felt immediately drawn to it. Kneeling down, he got a better look and noticed right away that the carvings on the stone's surface were not Egyptian. There were no hieroglyphs on it at all, in fact. But as he looked closer, hidden in the reliefs, he could clearly make out some curious runes that he didn't recognise.

On the side facing him, the carvings depicted a man reading from a book which emanated rays of energy out to a group of people who sat before him. Stephen had no idea what it meant, but it completely captured his interest.

"You interested? You buy?" the vendor asked.

Looking up at the man, Stephen did his best not to look too interested. "Maybe. How much?"

"For you? Seven thousand," the man said.

"Seven thousand?" Stephen asked incredulously.

"You mean Egyptian pounds, right?" Stephen's dad asked from behind him.

"Yes, yes," the trader said.

"That's like, three hundred British pounds," his dad whispered to Stephen.

"Oh," Stephen said. That didn't sound quite so bad, but it was still more than he wanted to spend. He didn't have three hundred on him, but he was curious to see what he could get the man down to. Maybe his dad would help him buy it. Looking back at the trader, Stephen thought before responding. "No, no. I can't pay that. How about, three thousand?"

"No. No way. Six thousand, maybe. Maybe."

Stephen liked bargaining, so he narrowed his eyes in a show of thought before answering, "Three thousand five hundred." The trader had dropped to six thousand easily, so he was clearly seeing what he could get away with. Stephen knew he needed to drive a hard bargain, but wanted to show he was willing to move.

The man thought about his offer. "Five," the man said.

"Three thousand, seven hundred and fifty," Stephen shot back, quick as lightning.

"Okay, okay, four thousand, but no less, that is last offer," the trader said.

That meant it was nearly two hundred for the item, which was still too much. Stephen looked at his dad, who whispered to him, "Agree to four, and I'll pay half." His parents had given him one hundred and fifty British pounds to spend in the market, so he'd still have some leftover, and Stephen was more than happy to share the item with his dad, who also looked interested in it.

Turning back to the trader, Stephen offered his hand. "Deal," he said.

The trader shook it, a broad smile lighting up his face. "Excellent, excellent. Here, I wrap, yes?" the trader offered while he and his dad sorted their money out and handed it over.

Taking the stone slab in his hands, Stephen was surprised how heavy it was. But holding it only cemented his idea that this was something special. He was sure he could feel it, the power that it contained. He couldn't wait to show it to his friends back home.

- Transcript from Witch trial of Francis Chastain

France, 1448

"Subject continued to wail and scream. Brother Macías was unable to bring forth any further details from the warlock. We deemed it necessary to use more coercive tactics and applied the use of the devices. The subject then began to talk. I asked the name of the witch who we had observed with him that night, but again he protested, saying he would rather die. He went on to say she would find him and make him suffer. We applied the devices again, and in time he offered us the name of Yasmin the Dark. Despite further applications of the tools, we could get nothing further from him, and he was placed in a cell. The following morning, Francis was dead. What little remained of him was splattered up one wall. The duty guard heard nothing all night, and no one had been granted entry."

Investigation

Cairo, Egypt

Vito scowled at nothing and everything. He might only be a little over a thousand miles from Rome, better than being over four thousand when he was in New York, but it was still too far for him, and the heat here was just ridiculous. It got hot in Italy, but nothing like this.

How did people live here?

That wasn't even the worst of it, though. There were far too many Muslims here for Vito's liking. Vito hated all other religions, including the many heathen variations of Christianity, for spreading their lies about what they thought to be the truth. Only the Vatican held the ultimate truth with their revered leader, Simon Peter, and the blessings of God that he and those others lucky enough to be graced by God's power could use.

But they weren't the only people with powers, and it was missions like the one he'd completed in New York that reminded him that the Devil's work was all around them.

The witch in New York had escaped him, and he had no idea which flight she'd boarded. They found out later of course, through their access to the airport security cameras, and had tracked the witch to Ireland, but they lost her somewhere in Donegal.

By then, though, Vito had been reassigned to a related case here in Egypt. But first, he'd stopped at the Vatican where he'd related the whole story to his mentor, Mary Damask. He'd cringed as he told her about his failure to apprehend the witch, Amanda. Mary could be a strict mentor when she wanted to be and had a harsh temper on her.

But it seemed like the trail was not yet dead. A report had come in from a priest in Cairo that a man had visited his church, raving about a demon he'd seen in the desert. The description of a huge black creature with a single horn matched that of the beast in New York. Not only that, but when Vito had visited the alleyway where the attack had taken place, he'd called on the grace of God to tell him more about the demon that had been there, and the main image he'd picked up was that of a dry, dusty desert.

Everything seemed to fit. This time, Vito was determined to succeed and follow the trail wherever it led.

He'd already visited the priest who recognised Vito as an official from the Vatican and had been incredibly helpful.

It seemed that the man, a Bedouin from the Sahara called Irfan, had arrived at the church in a state of distress. He was raving about a demon with a single horn who was hunting him. Further discussion had revealed that Irfan had stolen an artifact from an abandoned camp out in the desert. An artifact, which the man believed belonged to a demon who wanted it back.

Unfortunately, Irfan had said he'd sold it to a trader in the marketplace for a thousand Egyptian pounds, but that was all the priest had gotten from the man. He'd not pushed any further because the priest had no desire to hunt for the tablet. He was only interested Irfan's well-being.

An admirable position, but also entirely unhelpful in Vito's investigation. Luckily, the priest knew where Irfan was staying, so Vito had made his way over and now stood outside on the opposite side of the street, getting a good look at the building.

It was no good, though. He needed to have a look inside without attracting any undue attention, so he reached up for the cross that hung about his neck and offered a silent prayer to God Almighty. He felt the rush of divine power fill him up, and suddenly, he could see inside the building. He was looking at the inside of the dusty entrance and reception area, and if he looked back out through the front door, he could see himself on the opposite side of the street, leant up against a building to keep himself steady.

Using an extra set of eyes or ears could be disorientating.

Vito moved his vision and took a look at the open logbook on the other side of the counter. There was a computer too, but it was old and not turned on. Instead, the owner seemed to prefer pen and paper, which Vito was thankful for. A quick scan of the open book soon gave Vito all the information he needed. Irfan was two floors up. Vito also noticed that there was a note next to his entry listing the church as Irfan's benefactor for all charges.

Vito smiled and sent his senses straight up two floors and found himself in an empty room. Moving his vision sideways he went from room to room, looking for the Bedouin.

It didn't take him long to track the man down. He was sitting in a chair watching an old cathode ray tube television with an abysmal picture. The man looked tired and troubled but also unarmed.

Back on the street, Vito opened his eyes but left his senses where they were so he could keep an eye on his target. Vito crossed the road, taking care to dodge the horrific driving of the locals, and moved towards the entrance of the hotel. The key to getting past receptionists and such unchallenged was to look like you owned the place and knew where you were going. So, Vito ignored the man at the reception desk and made straight for the stairs and started up them unchallenged.

Half a minute later, Vito was approaching the door to the hotel room his senses were in, and so far, Irfan had not moved other than to adjust his position in the chair.

Not hesitating, Vito walked straight up to the door and gave it a solid kick, his strength fuelled by the grace of God.

The door slammed open easily, smashing against the wall as Vito strode in and slammed the door shut behind him. Irfan jumped out of his chair and looked up at Vito in shock.

"Who... who are you? What is the meaning of this?" Irfan asked in his native Arabic. Vito knew the language as well as any native and understood him perfectly.

"I'm here to ask you some questions," Vito answered, also in Arabic. "I'm a friend of the priest."

The man looked confused. "But, you broke down my door?"

"Just making sure you understand our relationship, Irfan. So, to be clear, you answer my questions, you don't ask me questions, understand?"

"But who are you?" the man asked.

Vito shot forward, moving quickly, and delivered a solid punch to the Bedouin's face, knocking him back onto the bed. The man yelped and groaned. Vito gave him a few seconds to recover before speaking again.

"I said no questions," Vito stated, having taken a few steps back to put some distance between them. With a quick, silent prayer to God, Vito reached back as if to remove something from his waistband and summoned his gun to his hand.

"Irfan?" Vito asked, but the man didn't answer. Instead, he suddenly got to his feet and made to lunge for Vito, but stopped partway when he saw the gun that Vito had pointed at him.

Irfan raised his hands in surrender and then sat back on the bed, a look of defeat spreading across his face. "Ask your questions."

"I only want to know one thing, where's the tablet you stole and subsequently sold? Who did you sell it to?"

***

"Stop, rewind that," Vito said, looking over the shoulder of one of the techs who worked for the Vatican. Several of them had been assigned to him as they hunted through hours of

CCTV footage from cameras all over Cairo, with a particular focus on the airport and main train terminals.

It was long, tedious work, but it had to be done. Vito watched them dispassionately as they scanned through the sped-up footage, hunting for family groups that matched the description that they had from the market trader.

Just like Irfan, the trader had opened up to Vito after very little pressure and described the family, including the blonde-haired boy of about sixteen years of age who had led the negotiations on the item's price.

Vito found it curious that the buyer had actually been the boy rather than the father, but he'd learnt a long time ago not to be surprised by the things he found out in this line of work.

So far, they'd tagged several groups of three who matched the look of the family they were hunting for, and as the techie moved the recording back, another group of three came into view, walking through the airport.

Vito gave the trio a good long hard look. They were the best match yet.

"Okay, follow them, they look right to me. Let's find out who they are," he said and set two of the tech guys to work. Within half an hour, he had the flight and the names of the family members in the video. As the tech guys followed them through the airport, they watched the boy, who they now knew was called Stephen, open up his hand luggage and lift out a large, heavy object wrapped in rags that fit the description of the artifact. The boy then went on to unwrap it enough to convince Vito that he'd found them.

Vito smiled at the screen with the frozen image of Stephen gazing in awe at the artifact he'd bought from the trader in Cairo.

"Successful hunt?"

Vito turned to see his superior and mentor, Mary Damask standing behind him. He'd not noticed her approach, but then he'd been so focused on the task at hand that he wasn't exactly surprised.

Mary was shorter than he was and sported a severe black bob haircut and a sharp face. She was a powerful woman, in more ways than one. Not least of which was the fact that she was the first, and so far, the only woman that had been appointed to the rank of Grand Inquisitor and been admitted into the Conclave. She was ambitious and calculating, and Vito felt reasonably confident that she had her eyes on the seat of Grand High Inquisitor, the highest rank within the Inquisition below Simon Peter.

"Very. I think we have our target."

"Excellent." Mary smiled.

- Notes on the Warlord Horlack and the Siege of Constantinople

By Kalmár the Elder, Scribe, and Poet

10th April 1204 *"The bloodlust of the demon Horlack was like nothing I had ever seen before during my time as the scribe of my master.*

I have seen many strange things in his employ, but what I saw that day chilled me to my very bones. This Horlack was like something from the Pit. Nothing could stand against it; it killed everyone in its path. Death has come to Constantinople.

May God have mercy on our souls."

Apprenticeship

Donegal, Ireland

Amanda stood balanced on one foot, her other foot tucked up beneath her, her knee turned out to the side, her hands held out wide as she let the feeling of Essentia flow through her. The energy filled her up, making her feel alive and vital, but also connected to everything around her.

These last few weeks had been filled with wonder and amazement every day as she learnt to harness and use her Magic under the careful tutelage of Gentle Water. She felt like she'd come a long way, and yet she knew the journey had only just begun.

Amanda balanced on top of what amounted to little more than a thick fence post. Arrayed around her were forty-nine logs, each one between six and ten inches in diameter—similar to the one she stood on—that had been rammed into the earth so that the tops of them were about three feet off the ground. They were spaced approximately two feet apart from each other in a rough circle which Amanda stood on the edge of.

Gentle Water stood on another post, on the opposite side, facing her.

"Ready?" Gentle Water asked.

Amanda opened her eyes, bringing her hand round before her, clenching her right hand into a fist and placing it into the palm of her other hand. She gave a slight bow to her mentor, indicating her readiness.

"Then we begin," Gentle Water said.

Amanda reached out with her mind, pulled on the ebb and flow of Essentia, and gave herself some added awareness by bending the forces of fate to her favour. With a smile, she hopped from one pole-top to the next with little effort, approaching her mentor. Within seconds, she was before him and defending herself against a punch, which she deflected.

It was like a dance, although one that was rife with danger and risk. One misstep and she would tumble between the poles to a rough landing. Something she had done a few times already. However, by using her Magic, she was able to keep an awareness of where the tops of the logs were and make sure she stepped on them and not between them. Amanda hopped from one to the next, deflecting Gentle Water's attacks and throwing her own back at him.

She was getting used to the apparatus now, having used it for several weeks, and was able to throw in the occasional kick as well. Gentle Water, though, was amazing to watch. His movements were graceful and precise, allowing him to move across the tops of the logs as if he were fighting on the ground.

Gentle Water pressed the attack, forcing her back and towards the edge of the circle. Amanda tried to move to the side to bring herself around him and give herself some room, but he anticipated her movement and blocked her, throwing strike after strike at her.

Seconds later, she found herself on the edge of the apparatus as Gentle Water sent one final punch at her.

Moments before it hit, Amanda sensed a surge of Essentia around Gentle Water as he pulled some of the local energy into him, and with her Magical sight, she could see the golden mist flow into his hand, making it glow before he threw his punch.

Gentle Water's fist caught her at the base of her ribcage. As the strike connected, the Essentia in his fist rushed into her.

They'd traded punches before many times in their sparring sessions, it was an accepted hazard of their training, but this one felt very different. Pain lanced through her body as if she'd been struck by a powerful electrical bolt and she felt a wave of nausea wash over her. Falling from the top of the log, Amanda landed on her back and had the air knocked out of her with a grunt of pain.

For a few seconds, she struggled to breathe before she finally sucked in some air and started to calm down. Her sternum ached like crazy, though. As she sat up, Gentle Water, who had already jumped down, knelt down next to her.

"Are you okay?" he asked, concern lacing his words. "I not hurt you too much?"

"You didn't, don't worry. Ugh, I'm grand, so I am," she reassured him. He hadn't really done any significant damage to her, but she felt sure she'd have a nasty bruise there later on. "What the bloody hell was that?"

Gentle Water smiled. "It Essentia Strike," he said. "Essentia can not only be used as fuel for Magic, but it can also be used for attack and defence. Concentrated Essentia, released suddenly through punch or kick, disrupt flow of Essentia through body. It hurt, yes? It also damage Aegis. Very useful."

She'd already learnt about the Aegis. Invisible to Riven humans, it was the Magical shield that all Magi used as their primary line of defence against Magic and harm. In its basic form, it was a hardened shell of Essentia around a Magi that protected them against Magical attacks. Any unwanted Magic thrown at the Magus would be deflected away by this barrier. An Aegis wasn't invulnerable though, as any Magical attack also damaged the Aegis, meaning it had to be maintained to keep functioning as protection.

Amanda was already capable of creating her own Aegis and had started to experiment with adding a force field element to it. Her basic Aegis would only stop Magic. A mundane, non-Magical bullet would pass right through it and still kill her unless she augmented the Aegis with further effects, such as a force field to deflect gunfire and other attacks.

"I think I'll have a nasty mark there later," Amanda said, rubbing the area he'd hit her.

"I heal you?" Gentle Water asked. Each time she'd been healed, she always thought back to that realisation that it was precisely what she could have done for Georgina. That she could have saved her friend. This idea haunted her even now, weeks later, even though she tried to put it out of her mind. But whenever she thought about it, she also remembered Gentle Water's words about using that pain. They were words that she had really taken to heart, and within hours of talking about it, she'd made a choice. She'd chosen to act. She didn't want to be passive anymore, she wanted to push herself and move forward. She felt a determination within herself, a slow-growing fire of passion and determination to make it on her own.

"No, no, I'll be fine," she said pulling herself up. He'd healed her a few times now when she'd hurt herself during their training. Seeing how the Magic he summoned could knit together cuts and make bruises fade to nothing was fascinating. He'd told her how all things had Essentia within them; it was a fundamental building block of the universe: the legendary fifth element, the Quinta Essentia, or Quintessence that Riven alchemists had theorised about for millennia. Inanimate objects all had Essentia within them. They had to, otherwise they wouldn't exist. But anything living, from humans to cats, right down to plants and trees, had a flow of Essentia moving through them. It was that flow that gave them life. The difference between a Riven and a Magus was that a Riven could not access that flow or control it. A Magus could, through their Anima Mundi, their life force, or, for want of a better word, their soul.

"So, tell me about this Essentia Strike," Amanda asked.

"Of course, follow," he said leading her through the clearing, away from the poles, and towards the tree line. "You pull Essentia to you, just like when you use Magic. You send it to fist, and when you hit, you release. When you hit living thing, Essentia in strike disrupt flow of Essentia through body, hurting them more," he said. "Watch."

They reached the edge of the clearing and Gentle Water walked over to a nearby tree. He dropped into a fighting stance. As she watched, she saw him work his Magic and the Essentia rush into him. The effect was always beautiful to observe. Usually, the golden mist hung in the air and flowed around lazily, occasionally rushing when something living passed by, creating small ripples or minor whirlpools. But Magic had a much more dramatic effect on it, making it surge and glow, creating powerful whirls and eddies in the mist. Just like it did now, as Gentle Water pulled the Essentia into his hand.

With her Magical sight, she could see his fist start to glow as the energy coalesced inside it, and then suddenly, he let his punch fly.

Bark and splinters of wood flew everywhere as his fist smashed straight through the side of the tree trunk. She also noticed the flow of Essentia through the tree judder and ripple, like the surface of a pond that had just had a stone dropped into it. The flow stabilised through the rest of the tree over the next few seconds, but the area around the broken trunk seemed eerily static.

"Wow, that was impressive, so it was," Amanda said.

"Essentia Strikes are powerful and primary weapon of Magi. You need to study this," he said.

"Of course, Gentle Water," she said and moved in to get a closer look at the tree.

"Are you thirsty?" he asked, wiping his forehead with his arm.

"I am, a bit," she said.

"I get us drink," he said and turned to walk away. "Practice, Amanda. Always practice," he called over his shoulder.

Looking down at her fist, Amanda took a calming breath and concentrated on pulling some Essenita into herself. She'd done it many times and found it almost second nature. Having a store of excess Essenita within you was always a good idea as a Magus. It turned your body into a battery and gave you quick access to greater levels of Magical energy for larger, more powerful effects. She could release it easily enough, too, but to release it through her fist in a sudden wave of power was something new to her.

With her fist glowing, she focused and released the Essentia, trying to make the whole lot rush out of her fist at once. It kind of worked. So Amanda tried it again, and again, and after several attempts, felt sure she had it.

Looking up at the tree, Amanda stepped over to it and narrowed her eyes. With a thought, she pulled the Essentia into her fist, making it glow in her Magical sight. And then, taking a deep breath, she flung her fist forward and released her Essentia.

Amanda's fist slammed into the tree trunk and came to a sudden, bone-crunching stop. She knew right away that she hadn't done it right. The sound of her bones snapping and the incredibly intense pain that exploded in her hand told her everything she needed to know.

Her legs started to wobble as she pulled her hand away from the tree and looked at it. It was a mess. Several bones had broken and were sticking out of the ripped skin as blood flowed from the wounds. Her fingers either wouldn't move correctly, or at all, and the pain was beyond anything she'd ever felt.

As she looked at her hand, she dropped to her knees and let out a shriek of anguish. Suddenly, a wave of nausea swept over her, and she heaved her breakfast onto the grass before dizziness overtook her and everything went black.

***

Opening her eyes, Amanda found herself on her bed in her cottage as the fog of unconsciousness faded away.

She felt groggy, but was slowly coming to her senses. As clarity started to return, a dull ache grew in her hand, and she suddenly remembered the idiotic action she'd taken by punching a tree with all her strength.

She lifted her hand and took a look at it, expecting to see a bandage or scars, but instead, her hand looked as good as new, as if nothing had ever happened to it. Amanda raised her eyebrows. She closed her fingers and made a fist before releasing it. There was stiffness and an ache there, but it was fading fast.

Gentle Water walked into the room carrying two glasses of water.

"Aaah, you awake. How you feel?" he asked.

"Um, I think I'm fine, actually," she said. "Sorry, that was a silly thing to do."

"It is understandable. No harm done, and you okay."

"I am," she agreed, sitting up fully and swinging her legs over the side of the bed. She flexed her hand once more before taking the glass from him. Her grip seemed unchanged, and by now, even the ache had gone. If she didn't know any better, she would have thought she'd dreamed it. "You Ported us here?" she asked, using the Magi word for teleportation.

"Yes," he answered with a smile. "I leave you for moment, have rest, feel better," he said as he walked out the room.

Taking another sip of her drink, Amanda sat back against her headboard and flexed her hand again, holding it up before her. The world was full of wonder and Magic now, literally so. Her ability with Magic had progressed to the point where she knew exactly what time it was and where on the earth she was at any given time, and she knew she'd only been unconscious for a few minutes at most. But in that time, Gentle Water had Ported them from the clearing back here and Magically healed her hand before going to get them a couple of drinks.

She shook her head in astonishment. She wondered if she'd ever get used to this. She also felt incredibly grateful to her mentor for healing her yet again. She was lucky to have him.

It kind of reminded her of Howie, and how he'd taken her in during her time of need a couple of years ago. She'd run away from the orphanage at seventeen, having finally had enough of their rules and with a desperate need to see the world. Somehow, following a series of lucky breaks, she'd managed to stow away on a cargo ship bound for New York. Back then, she'd taken it in stride, although she'd also recognised just how lucky she'd been. Now, though, as a Magi and knowing that her Magic had manifested as luck and good fortune for her and those close to her before her Epiphany, she had a new perspective on things.

Her successful trip across the Atlantic was almost certainly due to her unconscious Magic. But even with that luck, it didn't mean she'd had an easy time of it. Her good fortune only took her so far.

Once in New York, her money soon ran out, and within days she was sleeping rough with the other homeless. She'd curl up on benches or beneath elevated roads, but she often got moved on or came into conflict with the other guys out there on the streets.

Eventually, she ended up finding a large stoop in front of an apartment building that had a little corner that was somewhat out of view and not in the way of the residents. It had been created by an air conditioning and heating unit that stuck out into the upper level of the stoop. At night, her alcove was hidden enough to be dark, and she could curl up there beneath boxes and other rubbish she'd collected. If she was lucky, the fan in the unit she was next to was on and would kick out some heat. She got her best night's sleep there since she'd been forced onto the streets.

Some of the residents noticed her and gave her dirty looks, including a large, broad-shouldered black guy with close-cropped hair. About a week into her stay on the stoop, the rain came thundering down and even though she was under cover, she was still cold and damp and sat there shivering.

The black man ran up from the street and shook off his coat under cover of the ledge above the stoop, his eyes flicking up at her for a moment.

She watched him closely, her fingers on the shiv she'd made after waking up in the subway one night to find a man standing over her, his hands between her legs, and pawing at her chest. She'd kicked that attacker before running from the subway, and the next day made herself the knife from a shard of rusty metal.

The building's resident went to head into the apartment, but hesitated, teetering on the edge of indecision for a moment, nearly heading inside a couple more times before he stepped back out and moved closer to her.

"Hey, um, I was wondering if you wouldn't mind…" he started.

Anger flashed within her, and she interrupted him. "No, I won't fecking move on, you bloody gobshite. It's lashing down and it's feckin' freezing. Now, piss off," she blurted out.

The man raised his hands and recoiled from her outburst. "I'm sorry, I didn't mean to offend you, but, yeah, it's cold, so I was wondering if you wanted to come in and get a hot chocolate or something?"

Amanda was stunned by the man's offer and just stared at him for a good few seconds. Suddenly, tears filled her eyes as emotion got the better of her.

"I'm sorry, what did you say?" she asked, suddenly unsure if he'd actually said what she thought he'd said.

He'd repeated his offer to her again with a warm smile, and gestured into the building.

"Oh, um, sure," she said, before hesitating and gripping her weapon again. She'd frowned at him then. "You'd best not try any funny business; I have a knife, you know," she warned him, flashing the shiv.

But Amanda needn't have worried. His name was Howard Galton, although he insisted she call him Howie, and his intentions towards her were entirely honourable. They'd ended up sitting on his sofa, drinking hot chocolate, munching on cookies, and were soon deep in conversation. They'd got along famously, and when the end of the night came, he offered her his sofa for the night.

Within days, she'd moved into his spare room and they were on their way to becoming good friends. Howie was a doorman at a local nightclub called The Dark Side of the Moon, and she was soon spending some of her evenings there and getting to know some of the regulars.

Her life had changed dramatically over the course of just a few days. In many ways, Howie had saved her, not unlike Gentle Water had today, and in a more profound way several weeks ago when he'd taken her on as his apprentice.

Of course, looking back now, she wondered how big a part her Magic had played in that lucky break with Howie.

She supposed she'd never know.

- From the book, 'A history of the Dark Nomads' by Trevelyan

The earliest known record of Yasmin the Dark comes from the legend of Red Yasmin in northern Italy around nine hundred years ago. An eyewitness reported seeing Yasmin, a known local girl of about thirteen years, walking through the town in the dead of night, covered from head to toe in blood. She was never seen again after that, but her parents and three brothers were found mutilated in their family home—their chests cut open and their hearts ripped out. A set of bloody footprints, clearly those of a child, led out of the house and into the night. It was said that Yasmin was beaten and abused as a child, and the villagers distrusted the family due to their violent ways. Many locals thought they'd received their just desserts. The hearts of Yasmin's family were never found.

Visits

Rome, Italy

Raphaella sat on the edge of the bed and pulled the stocking the rest of the way up her leg before clipping the ends of the garter belt to the top of it. Satisfied with how it looked, she pulled on her underwear last so they could be removed quickly and easily without needing to remove the stockings. She looked at herself in the mirror and smiled, knowing that her visitor, who was due to arrive in about ten minutes, would be thrilled with how she looked. Picking up her nun's habit from the bed, she slipped into it, hiding the lingerie. She'd had the robes made with a hidden zip at the front so she could remove it easily, as well as open it slightly to allow cheeky glimpses of what was beneath.

Her body was just one of many methods she used to get the information she wanted. It was also the most fun way. She could use her Magic, of course, to pluck the answers she and her mistress needed from the heads of her victims, and often did, but there was a risk involved with that where the Vatican was concerned, and it didn't serve to corrupt those she wanted in her debt, either.

Raphaella stood at five foot seven, although the heels she wore added a few inches to that. She wore her jet black hair long with a severe fringe, and just for tonight, ruby red lips that glistened in the hotel room's harsh light. She twisted to the left and right, checking herself in the mirror one last time. Satisfied, she went into the small living area attached to the bedroom and sat down on one of the chairs beside the window that looked out over the city. In the distance, she could make out the Vatican easily. It was lit up like a gaudy Christmas tree by hundreds of lights and positively glowed. She'd be back there later, she thought.

Suddenly, Essentia surged close by, and with a whip-crack of rushing air, two figures appeared in the room with her.

She looked up, surprised, before quickly standing and fixing her eyes on the floor in deference once she saw who it was. "Baal Yasmin, I had no idea you were coming to see me tonight. To what do I owe the pleasure?" she asked, using the required honorific for her mentor and superior.

"Raphaella, it's always a pleasure to see you," Yasmin purred, her voice languid and sensual. "How is life in the Vatican?"

Raphaella looked up at her mistress. Yasmin was stunning. She was tall, perhaps about six foot with a lithe, taut body that was clad entirely in a shiny, black, form-fitting outfit. Only her hands and face were uncovered. The edges of the outfit she wore looked like liquid with runnels of black reaching down onto her hands and up her neck. Falling from her shoulders and billowing over the ground was a black mist that she wore like a cloak, the effect was quite intimidating.

Focusing on her face, Raphaella enjoyed the rather cruel beauty of her mistress. She was a good-looking woman, striking really, and looked like she was made from harsh straight lines. There was little about Yasmin that looked soft or kind.

The woman behind Yasmin was Kez, Yasmin's personal assistant and closest confidant. She ran errands for Yasmin and generally got her hands grubby doing the dirty work for her mistress. Kez sported a long ragged, patched-up, layered cloak that covered her entire body with a voluminous hood that looked like it had been worn for centuries. She was pale with thin, off-white hair, somewhat oversized eyes, sharp features, and two scars that ran parallel from her hairline, down through her eye sockets to her jaw. Together, the pair were a terrifying sight, not least because Raphaella knew just how powerful Yasmin was.

"Life is good, thank you, my Baal," Raphaella said. She wondered how long this meeting might be—she didn't want Yasmin scaring off her visitor.

"I wanted to hear more on the report you made about the Inquisitor visiting New York," Yasmin said.

"But of course," she said. She'd only sent in the report a few days ago, so Raphaella had wondered if this visit might be related to that, but this was unusual. If Yasmin was curious about some detail or other, usually Raphaella would get either a request for clarification or, on rare occasions, she might get a visit from Kez or one of the other Nomads in Yasmin's Dark Knights Coven. For Yasmin herself to visit meant there was something significant in there that required her personal attention. "Mary Damask sent Vito De Luca to investigate a report by someone that they had seen a demon in an alleyway in New York. The assumption the Inquisition made was that a young Magi had summoned the demon. Naturally, the Inquisition's bias led them to certain conclusions, but it does seem that a Scion attacked a girl, possibly a Magi, in an alleyway. We don't know why," she said.

"But that wasn't all, was it?"

"No, the Inquisition had a good description of the girl, who they believed to be a witch, to use their terminology. So, they were monitoring the transport hubs and found her at JFK airport. Their asset, Vito confronted the witch, but she got away."

"So, what do we know about this witch? The description mentioned red hair," Yasmin stated. Raphaella noticed how Yasmin was watching her very carefully, listening intently, but keeping her face completely neutral, never betraying any emotion at all.

"That's right. The report described her as having long, bright red hair and was of a slim but busty build. She stood out, in other words. I have a little more information on her now, though, which would have been in my next report to you. From interrogations that Vito carried out on her friends in New York, they know her name to be Amanda-Jane Page."

As she said the name, she noticed Yasmin's eyes widen ever so slightly—the first and barest trace of genuine emotion that Yasmin had displayed during her visit.

"You're sure of this?" Yasmin asked, relaxing again slightly, looking away from Raphaella in thought.

"Absolutely, it wasn't the name she used on her passport, though, on her flight to Ireland, that was…"

"I know what that was," Yasmin interrupted her. She turned back and smiled. "Raphaella," she said, and stepped in close, taking Raphaella's jaw between her fingers and thumb. "Thank you, you have done well," she said and kissed her on the lips. A long, slow, but gentle kiss before she pulled away.

"My pleasure, my Baal," Raphaella answered. Energy surged through the room once more, and with another snap of air filling the void they left behind, the two women were gone, leaving Raphaella alone.

Raphaella raised her eyebrows. She wasn't sure what that was about, but it sounded like this Amanda meant something to Yasmin. Whoever it was, Raphaella did not envy the girl.

Moving to a nearby mirror, Raphaella checked her make-up, and with a quick working of Magic, removed the smudge of lipstick from the kiss.

There was a sudden knock at the door. Raphaella smiled, this would be her visitor. Walking around, she unlocked the door and swung it wide, making sure to part her robes and show off her lingerie as she did so. The man on the other side of the door looked down at her, taking in her long slender legs and the swell of her breasts with a hungry lick of his lips.

"Oh, my child, you look radiant," he said.

Raphaella smiled. It seemed her outfit had indeed had the desired effect. "Thank you," she said. "But I'm even better to touch. Please, won't you come in, Cardinal?"

***

Lucian walked along the dull concrete corridor of his Sepulchre with Raal by his side. He was still annoyed by Ekua's outburst in the meeting earlier today, but it was just another in a long line of insubordinate comments and actions by his coven mate. One day, Ekua would need to either act on his clear dislike of him or shut the fuck up.

Apart from that, though, the meeting went well. There had been no further issues or incursions by Arcadian Magi since the report that his mentor, Nymira had given him recently. The event had gone unnoticed by Lucian and his people it was so subtle, but it seemed like the Inquisition had heard about it and sent in one of their men to check it out. Apparently, someone had been attacked in an alleyway by a rogue Scion. Unfortunately for the Scion, that person had gone through their Epiphany during the attack and blown the stupid fuckin' monster to hell. Serves the fucker right, he thought, brushing a stray dreadlock out of his eyes. According to Nymira's sources in the Vatican, the girl had skipped town.

Just as well, really, he thought. He couldn't be bothered with inducting someone into the Nomads right now, he was just too busy with other things and didn't want to deal with some mewling whelp who would probably dislike the way he worked.

Whatever. He didn't give a fuck. He had operations to coordinate, product to shift, supply lines to manage, and a nightclub to run.

Sometimes, he wondered if he hadn't taken on more than even he could handle, but he was the 'King of New York', so it came with the territory.

Lucian reached the corridor that led to his private quarters and strode down it.

"What does that mon think he doin', saying stupid shit like dat? Me got too much shit to be dealing wit these days without a batty hole like him fucking tings up all da time," he complained, his strong Jamaican accent colouring his words.

Raal didn't answer, but that was fine with Lucian; he was just venting anyway. He needed to have a rant to get things off his chest so he could concentrate on the night ahead.

The club, which was a few floors above where they were right now, had opened and people were already drinking and dancing. Lucian didn't usually get involved with the details of managing The Pit, leaving that to his Riven subordinates instead, but he always liked to have a general overview of how things were going.

Reaching the door to his private quarters, Lucian walked in followed by Raal, who closed the door behind him. The place was dark and unlit for the most part.

An awareness that someone wanted to talk to him through one of his mental Links blossomed to life in his mind. Lucian, like most Magi, had established Mental Links with all of his coven, even Ekua, so that they could communicate telepathically with each other over great distances. Once a Link had been made, you need only send out a request to the person you wanted to speak to, and provided they accepted the Link, you could talk using only your thoughts. Such Links didn't allow either Magi to bypass the others' Aegis with their magic, though, so it didn't compromise either Magi's defences to have a Link with someone.

The Link request was from Aneurin Maddox, the most computer savvy of Lucian's coven. ~*Whaa gwaan?*~ Lucian asked through the Link.

~We have an Aegis breach. Someone just punched a hole in it without breaking a sweat,~ Maddox replied, stress and worry evident across the link.

~When did this happen?~ Lucian asked.

~A few moments ago. I'm with Lex. We're trying to hunt them down now,~ Maddox explained.

"Lucian, it's such a pleasure to see you again," someone said.

Lucian turned to look in the direction of the sensuous feminine voice as Raal reached for a light switch.

Lucian didn't need to see, however. The voice was one he'd heard before and knew well. The illumination from the light in the kitchenette that Raal had turned on only confirmed it.

Yasmin's slender form stood in the dusky light of the living space. She lowered herself onto his sofa and crossed her lithe legs, as she looked at him from beneath her long, dark, wavy hair, shot through with an occasional purple streak.

~Cancel the alert, I have it under control,~ Lucian sent through the Link before closing it and silencing Maddox's protests. Lucian didn't want to have to deal with anyone else right now; not with a potentially hostile Arch Magus sitting on his sofa. This wasn't the first time he'd met Yasmin and of course, he, like most Nomads, knew the stories of her. The situation was precarious, he didn't want to appear weak and yet, he certainly didn't want to piss Yasmin off. That would be a death sentence for him. Just have to let it play out, he thought.

"The pleasure is all mine," Lucian said. "How can I help you tonight?"

Yasmin spread her arms over the back of the couch. "Oh, it's quite simple, really. Just lower your Aegis and let me have a look inside that head of yours."

"Excuse me?" Lucian asked, not quite sure if he'd heard her right.

"I'm not going to repeat myself, Lucian," she stated, her voice flat and even.

To his right, Raal moved. Lucian's apprentice drew his double-ended sword in a threatening motion. "He will do no such thing," Raal spat in anger.

"And who is this?" Yasmin asked Lucian, pointing casually at his coven mate.

"Raal," Lucian said in a low warning tone to his apprentice. But Raal ignored him.

"I'll show you who I am," Raal said, and sprinted forward, slashing his blade through the air before him.

Yasmin lifted a finger. The Essentia she shifted was intense and suddenly Raal flew backwards across the room, slamming into the back wall a good four feet above the ground and stayed there.

"You must learn to control your attack dogs, Lucian," Yasmin advised. "Now, what's it to be? Comply willingly, or make me do it by force. Either way is fine," she told him.

Lucian closed his eyes. He knew he had no choice. She could kill him in a second if she liked, and frankly he wanted to live another day, so with a sigh he cancelled his Aegis. "Go ahead," he offered.

Essentia flared. Suddenly, the whole world turned white and his mind was flooded with intense pain. It felt like an intense migraine that made his head feel like it was going to explode.

He had no idea how long it went on or what Yasmin was doing in his head. The screaming pain seemed to last forever and rendered him utterly incapacitated.

Then it ended as quickly as it had begun and Lucian found himself on his knees in the middle of his living space. Yasmin was gone, and Raal lay crumpled on the floor, alive but unconscious. The last remnants of the pain in his head faded away, leaving only a throbbing migraine.

He still had no idea what Yasmin had been looking for, but as long as she didn't return for another go, he couldn't care less. He did not want to go through that again.

- Notes from a speech by Louisa Hunt, Magi Scholar from the Ordo Obscura coven.

The barrier stopping us from crossing into the Aetheric Realm is as strong as it ever was. It seems the Earth's spirit world will be forever barred to the Magi after being so cruelly taken from us by the Archons.

Of course, the Nomads and other Magi continue to taunt us with stories of those who have made the crossing, but we in the Ordo Obscura will need to see some concrete proof before we agree that anyone has managed to do the impossible.

One story that continues to raise its ugly head is that of Shaitan, the Nomad who is most famous for apparently crossing into the Abyss and returning, although, where is he now? No one knows. I personally think it's more likely it's a hoax and he never even existed.

We may be called Arcadians, but I have my doubts we will ever return to the fields of Arcadia.

Body and Spirit

Donegal, Ireland

"I must say, Amanda, I impressed with progress. You come long way in very short time. You already strong in Magic when I meet you, but you learn in months what takes others years. You officially rank of Knight now," Gentle Water said.

Amanda couldn't help the smile that played over her face. She wasn't quite sure how to handle the compliments other than to thank him, but to know she'd come so far in what was apparently an impressively quick time was thrilling.

Gentle Water had talked about the ranks of Magi before. Apparently, you started off as an Apprentice, before moving onto being an Adept, then a Knight, a Sage, a Master, and then finally an Arch Master. Gentle Water had explained there were very few Arch Masters, and they were incredibly powerful and old. He'd also said that reaching the rank of Master was pretty much impossible inside of an average human lifespan, only those Magi who were long-lived or immortal could attain such ranks.

Needless to say, Amanda wasn't thinking that far ahead anyway, she was having fun at her current level, and Gentle Water was still teaching her new things and showing her what she could actually do with her Magic.

"I couldn't have done it without you, though," Amanda said warmly to her mentor. They were sitting inside the cottage close to the warm fire. It was morning, and the cottage was still heating up. She'd heard Gentle Water moving about the place, so she'd climbed out of bed and curled up with a mug of cocoa in one of the chairs in the living room in front of a roaring fire. Gentle Water sat in another chair a few feet away, sipping his own drink.

"Thank you. You would have done well with any mentor, Amanda, but it is honour to have you as apprentice," he said.

"So, what's the plan for today, then?" Amanda asked, taking a sip from the mug she held in both hands.

"Later, we go for walk. There is place local to here that I show you, but before, I want talk to you about body Magic," he explained.

"Oh, okay," Amanda replied.

"Remember I heal you before, yes?" he said.

"Of course," Amanda answered.

"That just using magic to make body back to original state, but Magic can do more. Magic can enhance, transform beyond anything imaginable. From simple spot and blemish removal to making body stronger, faster, tougher. Maybe have vision of cat or eagle or both? Can transform into other people. Man, woman, anyone, even animal, or anything you imagine," he said.

Amanda's eyebrows had risen halfway up her forehead as he'd spoken. She couldn't help but imagine the possibilities. The limit of Magic it seemed, once she was of a rank high enough to do these things, was literally her imagination. It was like wish fulfilment. She could potentially have anything. She'd learnt some time ago that Magi had little use for a job or other ways of acquiring money when, with a quick working of Magic, she could conjure as much cash as she needed. But then, why would she need money when she could conjure anything she wanted from thin air, anyway?

Amanda was still getting used to this profound mental shift in what she could actually do.

Thinking through what Gentle Water had said, though, she thought it would be fun to spend a day as a man sometime, or perhaps as an eagle soaring over the Earth. She could experience all kinds of wondrous things.

As she absent-mindedly rubbed her face, her finger played across a spot on her face, and Gentle Waters words suddenly resonated through her mind.

"So, I could spend a moment in the mirror each morning and remove spots and things?"

Gentle Water nodded. "You can, yes, but if you enhance appearance, be careful, it easy to take too far, and look quite strange. It happen many time before."

Images she'd seen in the tabloids of plastic surgeries gone wrong flashed through her mind, and she understood right away the pitfalls of such Magic.

"I understand," she said, finishing her drink. "Let me go and get ready, a walk sounds like just what I need."

She was soon looking at her skin in the harsh, unforgiving light of the bathroom mirror and studying her face. There were several blemishes she wanted to get rid of, not least of which was the unsightly spot that sat on her chin, all red and angry. Calming herself, Amanda concentrated and started to will

Essentia to bend to her desire and as she watched, the spot faded away to nothing.

Reaching up, Amanda touched her face where the blemish had once been, and sure enough, it was gone.

"Hah, crazy," she said to herself.

She couldn't help but smile at this wonderful revelation as she got herself into the shower.

She was soon dressed and back out in the main cottage where Gentle Water was waiting for her.

"Are you ready for walk?" he asked.

"Of course," she said, following him out of the house as he started to make his way north rather than east towards the forest.

"So, with all the Magi able to change and enhance their bodies and appearance, are any of them fat or ugly?" she asked. It was something that had occurred to her in the shower—most Magi, she guessed, would look young and at least reasonably good looking, if not outright beauties. Surely, no Magi would live their life as a morbidly obese person if they could just make it disappear with a thought?

Gentle Water smiled. "Hmm. Most are attractive." He shrugged.

"Okay, figures," Amanda said, even more curious to meet other Magi and to see what they looked like.

Continuing on, they were soon over the hill and moving through the Irish countryside, keeping their distance from the occasional house or cottage they could see.

"So, in few days, I take you to my coven, The Legacy, in Paris," Gentle Water said to her in a conversational tone.

"What? Paris? Oh, wow, excellent," she said. "I've never been to Paris before."

"I'm sure you will have good time," he said.

"You bet," Amanda answered. Gentle Water had spoken to her about his coven before. She knew they were based in Paris and were involved in supporting smaller covens across Europe from those who would harm humanity. She'd wanted to go there sooner, but Gentle Water had said that she was better off learning her craft here, somewhere familiar to her so that she could concentrate better and focus on her learning before becoming distracted by the bright lights of the city and the new experiences that the Legacy would offer her.

She understood, but she'd been aching to go and meet more Magi for months now.

"Royston tell me that there will be party, or ball in Paris that you can go to," he said.

"A ball? Like a cocktail party?"

"Correct."

"Well then, I'll need a suitable dress," she mused. She guessed she would be able to go shopping in Paris for that, though, so she wasn't too worried. Instead, she was just thrilled and excited that she would finally get to see more of the world. She felt sure that another reason why Gentle Water was keeping her here was to protect her. By staying in rural Donegal, they could remain relatively hidden and not get involved in any trouble.

As they crested the next hill, Amanda found herself looking down into a lush, verdant valley, at the bottom of which was an ancient stone circle that seemed entirely untouched by modern hands.

It was an impressive sight, but there was more going on here, too. Amanda could feel a surge in the local Essentia here, like a rushing of power that had started to ripple through her as she'd climbed the hill.

With a quick and simple thought, Amanda pushed her vision into the Magical spectrum, and suddenly the vista before her changed. Not too far away, to her left, was a fast-moving current of Essentia surging through the air and rushing past her, off over the top of the standing stones where another river of energy, the same as the one closest to her, crossed its path. Where they intersected directly above the stone circle, the Essentia glowed with a strength and brightness she could practically feel. Looking closer, she could see the golden glowing Essentia here starting to stick together and drip like lava from the rivers of energy to collect in a pool, right where the stone circle was.

"What is this place?" Amanda asked.

"The Essentia streams are ley lines, rivers of Magical energy that go all around world. Where they cross, becomes Pooling. Reservoirs of Essentia. Magic is easier here, and barrier to Abyss, thinner."

Gentle Water's teachings had covered the basics of the Spirit World or the Aetheric Realm as it was more properly called, as opposed to the Material Realm which they were in now. The Aetheric Realm was separated from the material world by a barrier called Acheron, or more commonly, the Null Realm. Millennia ago, the Magi were able to cross that barrier and visit the land in the Aetheric Realm, which the Magi had once called Arcadia, but it was cut off from the Magi by the Archons when they retreated to their fortress to sleep away the centuries. The formerly beautiful Arcadia was slowly corrupted and transformed by the Archons' continued presence and turned into a hellish landscape known as the Abyss.

Few had ever seen it, let alone visited, but the stories of people making the crossing were many. The closest a Magi could get to the Aetheric Realm now was to make small realms, Null Realms within the barrier of Acheron itself, but they were difficult to make and harder to maintain.

The only other alternate realm that she'd learnt about was Sheol or the Land of the Dead. Where you went when you died. Or, more accurately, where your Anima or life force went. She hadn't learnt much about that place but did occasionally wonder if Georgina and Stuart might be there. For now, the loss of her friends was still too raw, but maybe one day she would take a look there.

"It's amazing," she said, looking out at the surging forces of Magic and feeling their life-giving properties. Being so close to the ley line was a thrilling experience.

"It seems like the world has doubled or tripled in size these last few months," she said. "There's so much that I'd love to explore."

"One day, maybe. Also, there is outer space," he said, pointing up.

Amanda blinked. "You mean, there are Magi in space?" she asked, slowly looking up into the azure sky.

"Indeed. They are the Nexus. Magi have been out there for thousands of years," he said.

"Wow," Amanda said. "I'd love to go there too."

"One day. But one thing at time. Let us stay here on ground for time being, yes?"

Amanda took a breath and let it out slowly. Gentle Water was right. She was getting way ahead of herself here. The idea of visiting other realms and deep space was a lovely ambition to have, but her home was here, and she was only really just learning of the endless potential of the magical world around her. Taking things slowly, one step at a time, and staying grounded at least for the time being, was probably a wise idea.

"Shall we run through some Magic?"

"Sure," Amanda said brightly, turning to her mentor. They did this most days now, running through some of the more common effects that she would be using, getting them to be second nature to her.

Suddenly, without warning, Gentle Water unleashed a minor bolt of Essentia at her. It wouldn't seriously hurt her, but they could sting like crazy, and she knew he did it for a reason. One of the most basic workings of Magic was the ability to create a shield. The Magi referred to them as an Aegis, and they were basically hardened Essentia that a Magus would surround herself with to protect her from Magical attack. Out of everything she'd learnt, this one effect could save her life more than anything else, or so Gentle Water had been keen to drill into her. He'd taken to throwing Essentia bolts at her at entirely random moments, such as over breakfast, or when they were watching TV. It felt like a game at times, but Amanda knew its true and life-saving purpose.

Gentle Water's bolt of Magical energy harmlessly hit Amanda's Aegis that had been in place since waking up and dissipated quickly.

"Excellent. Now, Link with me," he said.

Concentrating again, Amanda wished a connection to Gentle Water into existence, linking her mind to his. He accepted it, creating the Link. With another thought, she sent a pulse of thought along the Link, effectively letting him know she was trying to contact him. He smiled and opened the Link.

~Thank you, Amanda,~ he sent to her through the Link. ~Now, fetch me my coffee mug from the Cottage.~

"Sure thing," she replied aloud, concentrating again on being in the cottage rather than here. The Essentia around her swirled and rushed into her, and with a flash of light behind her eyes, she found herself in the kitchen of the cottage. She spotted her Mentor's mug, picked it up, and Ported back to him, appearing in the same spot she'd stood two seconds before, except she was holding his mug.

Gentle Water smiled. "Excellent work."

"Hold on," she said, and worked her Magic again, Porting the mug back to the cottage without her. It disappeared from her hand with a *thwip*.

"Impressive, most impressive."

Amanda smiled. "Thank you, Darth Vader."

Gentle Water frowned in confusion.

"Forget it," Amanda said, waving away his unvoiced question.

He shrugged. "Okay, that enough for now."

"Okay," she answered and turned back to the vista before her. "I think I'll just sit here awhile and enjoy the view. It sounds like my life is about to get a good deal more complicated in the weeks to come."

- Excerpt from an Interview with a top Nephilim Model.

It sounds like Nephilim has really changed your life.

It has. Since joining the Nephilim Modelling Agency, my life has become like something you read about in fashion magazines. I travel the world and meet some of the most fabulous people ever. It's great.

We saw you out with (Censored) the other night in Milan. Anything going on?

Oh, you know, we met at a party and hooked up for a wild night out. He's great, you know. Nothing like the media likes to portray him. He's filming another action film right now. He says he'll try to get me a part.

Really? Wow, You're really living the high life.

I really am. I mean, I grew up with nothing, absolutely nothing. We had no money, no new clothes, not even any makeup! Can you imagine me with no make-up on?

Do you see your family?

No, and I don't care to. They've brought me nothing but misery. Now, I have everything I could ever want—designer clothes, fast cars, anything.

Drugs?

Look, you have to fit in, you have to do what everyone else is doing. So what if there's some smack on offer at these parties? It helps you to have a good time, get over it.

Angel

Syndicate Island

"Excellent. Good work, Angel," Isha said to her from where he sat behind his desk. Isha was a youngish Indian man, somewhat attractive, and also Angel's manager. She hated him and his condescending attitude towards her. She desperately wanted to lash out and crack his head open on that ostentatious desk of his, but she didn't. Instead, she just smiled. Not that he could see it; he wasn't even looking at her.

"Thank you, sir," she said. "Is there anything else?"

"Just the usual cataloguing of the new Scion recruits. I'll send the files over to your office shortly," he said, waving his hand about impatiently, dismissing her.

Angel nodded, although she wondered why she bothered and made her way out of the office. She scowled at him through the windows as she walked by, wanting to reach out with her Magic and hurt him, but she resisted, as she always did.

He wasn't worth blowing this mission over, and if she started to throw her Magic around too much, he'd begin to suspect that she wasn't who she was supposed to be. It annoyed her, but she was making inroads with others who would better serve her needs anyway.

Stepping out of Isha's office, she walked along the corridor, noting the occasional admiring glances from some of the other people she passed, making a mental note of who was looking at her in case they might be useful to her later on. On her left, the wall of the corridor ended to be replaced with floor to ceiling plexiglass windows, giving her a magnificent view of the west side of the tropical island the complex was based on.

The Syndicate compound was massive, dominating this small privately-owned island that was conveniently not on any maps, and also well away from any shipping lanes. The weather out there was hot and humid, like most days, but the air-conditioned interior of the Syndicate complex kept the employees at a constant comfortable temperature.

She soon reached her office door and walked inside, seeing the new pile of files on her desk right away. Isha wasn't hanging around, it seemed.

Angel sighed. She knew it was a means to an end, but there were times when working undercover was a real drag.

She moved around her office, dropped into her cool, comfortable office chair and crossed her legs. These files weren't needed right away, so she could do the work anytime she wanted. She'd entered enough of these to know they were not a top priority.

Grabbing the computer mouse, she unlocked the screen with her password and checked the latest data mining program for results. She'd gotten a few more passwords out of it, which would give her access to a few more files that she shouldn't be able to see. She had a quick scan through them, but there was nothing about them that suggested that this data might give her any additional clues as to the whereabouts of the Lazarus Scroll.

Angel pressed her lips together in consternation and checked her private emails. She noticed the coded message from her coven right away and opened the email up to have a look at it.

From what she could understand from the code, it seemed that her coven had heard about a new artifact that both the Inquisition and Yasmin were hunting down. She wasn't much interested in what the Inquisition was after. They were always chasing after shadows, but Yasmin was a different matter altogether. If she was hunting something, then this would be a significant find. Yasmin didn't hunt down trivial artifacts.

Angel sat back and stretched one leg out, rotating her foot to stretch it as she thought this through. It had been a while since she'd been in direct contact with her coven, so it would be worth taking a trip back to Milan to make sure everything was running okay at Nephilim and to make sure her coven was behaving themselves. Plus, she felt like she needed a break anyway.

But that meant she needed to get a leave of absence approved, and she would need to use a plane. She hated the idea of sitting for hours on a flight when she was perfectly capable of Porting to Italy from here, but she needed to maintain her persona as an Apprentice Magi. She didn't want to raise any suspicions at this stage of her infiltration.

So, she thought through the people she was cultivating, and the only one that sprung to mind was Ian.

"Well," she said to herself. "Let's go pull some strings." Rising from her chair, she checked herself over in her mirror before leaving the office.

Angel was of average height with long blonde hair that fell over her shoulders. She was a businesswoman, both in her investigation of the Syndicate and in her usual life back in Milan running Nephilim Industries.

She'd taken what she'd wanted from other businesses and organisations before, and usually it was a quick, judicious working of Magic, and she was done.

The Syndicate was different though, and required a more subtle touch. Magi and Scions were everywhere within this shadowy group, and her cover as an apprentice Magus meant that there was little she could do Magically. If they suspected that she was a Sage-ranked Magus, her mission would be over.

But Angel considered herself a resourceful woman and was not above using her feminine wiles to get what she wanted. Seducing the Riven members of this group was child's play, especially with a little Magical nudge here and there.

Besides, people were weak, hormone-filled animals and it didn't take much to get them to give in to their more basic desires. All it took was a little push, and suddenly they were doing something that they knew they shouldn't and knew would get them into trouble. Her short, hip-hugging pencil skirt and thin, fitted blouse were more than enough to get most men, and a surprising amount of women, to give in to their desires.

Besides, it was fun.

She enjoyed choosing the cutest co-workers in the most advantageous positions, seducing them, and then blackmailing them to get what she wanted. She got to have some fun and move forward in her mission, all at the same time.

She used these little indiscretions wisely, recording them when she could so she could blackmail the target later. She had a few lower-level managers in her pocket already who were more than willing to do as she asked.

Ian was a new one and the highest up the chain she had dared go so far. She doubted she'd need to go any higher for now. He was only one step below the board of directors, and most of them routinely carried Magical items on them to protect themselves. She'd find one she could tempt at some point, but she'd need to avoid the Magi and Scions and keep to the Riven board members.

For now though, Ian would do.

She thought about what she could do and then smiled as a cheeky idea sprung to mind.

Ian's office wasn't far and was closer to the executive boardrooms. Setting off, she smiled at the few people she saw, until she reached the room Ian was in and knocked on the door that led directly into his office, ignoring the secretary's side room that was attached to it.

"Come in," he called. "It's open."

Angel opened the door and stood in the doorway, her hands behind her back.

"Good morning, Ian," she purred.

"Angel," he exclaimed, flushing slightly. "It's good to see you. How may I help you today?" He sounded nervous, but she couldn't blame him really.

"Oh, I need a favour," she said. "Nothing huge, but it needs approval from senior management."

"Oh, well, depends on what it is, really," he said, starting to regain his composure as he slipped back into his business voice.

With a quick thought, and working of Magic so minor and subtle that few would detect it, certainly not a Riven like Ian, she turned on the camera she had previously hidden in here and set it recording.

"Well, let me try and convince you," she said and flicked her hand out. Angel's underwear, which she had removed back in her office, flew through the air to land perfectly on the desk before him.

His eyes widened like plates as he looked down at the lacy black and purple panties.

"Aaaah…" he croaked.

"Sir, your ten-thirty just arrived," said the voice of his secretary through his phone. Ian cursed to himself and grabbed Angel's underwear off his desk as he looked up at her, clearly in a state of confusion as to what to do next.

Angel closed and locked the door behind her. The secretary was in the adjoining room, and couldn't see what was happening. Angel smiled at him and whispered. "Cancel it."

She saw him shift about in his seat uncomfortably, unsure what he should do.

"Unless you want your wife to see that footage I showed you," she said.

Ian stabbed the intercom on his phone. "Something's, um, come up. Get him to come back later. I'll need to have some time undisturbed in here," he said, and then cut off the link before his secretary could protest. He looked up, slightly angry at her now.

"Don't be like that," she purred. "I'm going to make this worth your while, believe me," she said as she reached the adjoining door to his secretary's office and turned the lock.

"What are you doing?" he asked.

"Making sure we're not disturbed," she said.

"Why?"

"I need authorised time off and a plane to Europe. Today."

"And why would I do that?" he asked.

Angel undid a button on her shirt. "You know why."

Ian sighed. "I could get into trouble over this."

"No, you won't. You're going to authorise that flight for me, and then… Well, we'll see, won't we."

She could see the cogs turning in his head, and as she pulled her shirt open further, revealing part of her bra, she could see his interest in her, and his arousal, grow. He was flushing a little too.

"Alright, hold on," he answered, and tapped away on his computer. Angel walked around his desk and watched him approve her request.

She smiled at him. "Thank you."

"So, how will you make this worth my while?" he asked.

She gave him a wicked grin. "How about I swallow?"

Ian gulped, blinking at the thought. "Yeah, alright, that would work."

***

Her phone pinged as Angel strode along the corridor, away from Ian's office having left him satisfied, but wanting more. The new file she'd recorded and saved to the cloud was another useful nail in his coffin, as well. Seducing these idiots wasn't the most efficient way for her to get what she wanted, but it did mean she could move about amongst the Magi within the Syndicate, unseen, and that was invaluable.

Checking her phone, the message alerted her that her plane was ready and waiting for her, so she made her way through the complex and out towards the private airstrip that the Syndicate maintained.

The money that the Syndicate controlled was incredible. They ran multinationals around the world and could influence governments and private corporations anywhere. All of it under the direction of the founder of the Syndicate, Mr Black.

Angel still wasn't exactly sure what the purpose of the Syndicate was, but they employed Riven, Magi, and Scion alike, building their empire and their control. One day she hoped to find out the truth, but until then, she'd keep building her power base and her library of blackmail material.

The flight to Italy was long and tedious, and just so much slower than Porting.

The moment she was clear of the plane, however, she Ported from the airport and appeared in her office in Milan. The room was exactly as she'd left it. She sat in her chair and enjoyed its familiar feel. If felt good to release the grip she kept on her Magic when she was on the Syndicate island. Keeping up the ruse of her being a mere Apprentice when she was nearing the level of Master was a lot of work. If she was finally able to find and lay her hands on the Lazarus Scroll, though, and discover what the Syndicate was involved in, then perhaps it would be worth it.

In her mind, the presence of someone wanting to open a Link with her suddenly made itself known. It was her coven mate.

~You're back. May I come in?~

~Of course,~ Angel answered.

Magic flared, and suddenly a girl of about six or seven years of age in a cute pink dress with flowers on it appeared in her office.

"Cherub," Angel smiled. "You sensed my return."

"Always, my Baal. I take it my report on the activities of Yasmin took your interest?" she asked in her sing-song voice.

Angel only smiled.

"Then I'll be happy to fill you in on the details we know. Our contact has informed us that Yasmin as made a rare trip to personally handle something that's come to light. He's still looking into it, but we know that it's linked to an artifact that the Vatican is chasing. We suspect that Yasmin is after the same thing. So, if Yasmin is handling this personally, I think we can assume this could be big."

"Do we know anything about what the artifact is?"

"Apparently, Yasmin had organised a dig in the Egyptian desert overseen by one of her younger apprentices, Amy Bergman. It seems that they not only found the artifact, but also woke something up which killed the entire dig team, Amy as well. The artifact is some kind of large stone slab and is now in the hands of a British family somewhere in London. It may be that Yasmin merely wants her property back, given that it was stolen from her dig, but I think there's more to it than that."

"An unknown artifact in London?" Angel said, thinking. "Well, there are only a few places in that city a Riven could take such an item if they wanted it identified."

- An old Diary entry of Emmanuelle Page, Mother Superior of St Mary's Orphanage

She's been gone for a week now, and there's no trace of her at all. The full extent of her planning has come to light, including the money she took from my office and the food from the kitchens. This wasn't some random teenage impulse; this was planned well in advance. We put the word out the moment we knew she'd left the premises and filed a missing person report with the Garda shortly after that, but she's long gone by now. She could be anywhere in the world if she were smart enough, and if I know Amanda as well as I think I do, then I doubt she'll be in Ireland anymore, and I have no idea if I will ever see her again.

Orphanage

Donegal, Ireland

It was a lovely, balmy day as Amanda walked up the driveway and approached the collection of buildings that loomed up in front of her. They were made from old black stone with green moss and lichen threading its way through the brickwork. The place looked like it used to be some kind of stately home, but the sign out front declared it to be the St Mary's Convent School and Orphanage of Donegal.

Amanda paused for a moment and just looked up at it. She had a lot of memories of this building, but returning to it after leaving at seventeen, after so much had happened to her, felt strange. She'd only really been away for a little over two years, but it seemed like a lifetime. The place felt different now. It was part of her past, not her future, but she couldn't leave for Paris without at least paying a visit. She felt like she needed some kind of closure on this chapter of her life, and she was also hoping that Alicia was still here.

That, of course, would be a long shot, but at the very least, she might be able to find out where Alicia had gone. Had she found a home somewhere, maybe? A family to take her in? Or perhaps she'd joined the convent. She'd said a few times over the years that she wanted to join the ranks of the sisters.

Whatever direction Alicia had taken, Amanda hoped to find out today.

Walking into the front entrance of the school Amanda found herself in the reception area. She'd seen it several times before, but it had not been a room she'd visited often.

Filled with well-cared-for seating, tables with magazines upon them, and pictures hanging from the wood-panelled walls, they clearly wanted to impress anyone who came here. The room gave the place a stately elegance and instilled a sense of history to the school, which had been here for quite a long time.

To her left, sitting behind a dark wooden desk was a woman in a beige cardigan buttoned all the way up, the collar of her white blouse folded over the top of the neckline.

She peered at Amanda over the rim of her glasses, which were perched on the end of her nose.

Amanda walked towards her and noted how the woman quite obviously looked her up and down with a disapproving sneer.

Amanda wore fitted, ripped jeans along with a white top with a smiling pumpkin stretched over her chest. She finished the look off with a denim jacket and a pair of sneakers.

The receptionist probably thought she looked scruffy, but Amanda didn't care. She felt comfortable, and that was way more important than what some self-righteous woman thought of her.

"Can I help you, dear? Are you lost?"

"I'm not lost. I was in the area and wanted to come and visit," she said casually.

"Well, I don't know what you think this place is, but you can't just waltz in here for a visit," she replied, her tone condescending.

"Sorry, I know, but I used to be a pupil here. I was an Orphan, and I… I moved out a couple of years ago," Amanda explained.

"Oh, so, one of our success stories," the woman said, her tone warming up a touch.

Amanda smiled. "I guess so."

"Well, this is a working school, so you can't just go wandering around. I don't know if there would be anyone available to come and see you, but take a seat, and I'll see what I can do."

Amanda thanked her, walked away from the desk, wandering between the furniture. After a moment, she spotted some annual school photos framed on the wall. She remembered posing for these each year with the entire pupil population of the school. They were always a welcome break from maths or whatever. Walking over, she noted the years on them and found the last one she would have been included in and started hunting for herself.

It didn't take long. She stood out from the crowd with her red hair. It took her a little longer to find the dark-haired Alicia, but she did soon enough and smiled at the memory. Hearing some movement behind her, she looked over to see a young man had walked in and approached the receptionist. They talked and looked in her direction. Amanda smiled and waved, which seemed to annoy the receptionist.

The young man started to head over to her. Amanda smiled, he was a good-looking guy, and she enjoyed watching him move. Part of her was quite tempted to flirt with him. It had been a while since she'd been with a man, and to be honest, although she was far from being a virgin anymore, she didn't really count any of her sexual encounters to date as anything meaningful. In fact, she usually just did her best to forget them.

As he approached, she caught his eye and held the look for a long moment, only for him to walk into the corner of a chair and hurt his leg. She smiled to herself. Slick, she thought.

"How are yeh? I'm Will," he said when he finally approached her, offering his hand.

"Will you?" Amanda joked.

"Um…" he said, unsure how he should answer.

Amanda smiled and shook his hand. "Sorry. Hi, I'm Amanda, nice to meet you."

"So, I hear you're a former pupil here?" he asked.

"An orphan, yes. I was in the area and thought I'd pop by, so I did. I lived here for seventeen years," she said.

"That's quite a while. So, you have a family now?"

"I suppose so. It's been a rocky ride, but I found my way," she said, catching him giving her an admiring glance. She smiled. Dragging him to the nearest broom cupboard for a quickie was an inviting thought, but she was here to see some old friends, not to have a quick ride with the first attractive man she laid eyes on.

"That's great. So, did you want to see anyone specifically?"

"Well, I'd like to go and see Emmanuelle Page and say hello, but that's over in the convent, so, I was just interested in remembering the way things were and seeing some familiar faces," she said.

"Well, we can't just go wandering about the school, but we could head over to the staff room and get a drink. Maybe you'll see someone there."

"Sounds good," Amanda smiled, and followed him out of the reception, along a few corridors, and into the staffroom. Will led her over to the coffee machine and poured her a drink. It wasn't very hot and it tasted a little bitter, but this was a teacher staff room, so she didn't complain.

"Is that you, Amanda?" said a man behind her. Turning around, she looked up into the kindly face of her old geography teacher, perhaps her favourite teacher.

The faculty was comprised of both teachers and nuns. The sisters taught religious studies and served as spiritual leaders while the regular staff filled in the gaps in the sister's knowledge, teaching the more specialised subjects.

Amanda never really liked any of the classes she had with the nuns, instead, always preferring the outside staff, with Mr Croft being her favourite.

"Mr Croft," she said with a smile. "I was hoping to see you."

"How come you're back here? Did you not have enough of us?"

"I was in the area and wanted to come say hi," she said.

"In the area? You've been gone for over a year."

"Yeah, I know, I do be thinking of you every day though, to be sure."

"So, don't hold out on me, did you get to New York?" he asked.

Amanda couldn't help the smile that spread across her face. "I did, it was amazing." She had no plans to tell him the truth of what had happened in New York. Instead, she stuck to telling him how wonderful she thought it was. She waxed lyrical for a while about the more fun aspects of New York and enjoyed the smile on Mr Croft's face.

They chatted and smiled for a while until she noticed someone walk in wearing a grey nun's coif, grey cardigan, skirt, tights, and very sensible shoes. She didn't look up at Amanda, but Amanda knew right away who she was.

Excusing herself from Mr Croft, she wandered over and came up next to the young woman, her heart fluttering with nerves.

"Alicia?" Amanda asked nervously.

The young woman looked up, and it took her about a second to realise who she was looking at.

"Oh, my goodness, Amanda. Is it you?" she asked.

Amanda smiled at her old friend. "It is," she said and quickly pulled her in for a hug. They embraced for a long moment before Alicia pulled away, tears streaming down her face. Amanda had started to tear up as well and sniffed them back. "Don't you get me started."

"I'm sorry, I just... I had no idea you were coming," Alicia said. "You just disappeared. Mandy. Oh, my gosh, it's great to see you. What are you doing here?"

Amanda sniffed. "Just visiting, for old times' sake, really."

"How long are you staying for?"

"I have a couple of hours, I think," she said.

Alicia steeled herself and sniffed back her own tears. "Okay, bear with me one moment, I'll get cover for my shifts," she said and disappeared off.

***

"I still can't believe you actually made it to New York," Alicia said. "People were looking for you for days. You have no idea what chaos you caused."

"I'm sorry, I am, but I had to do it. I was dying here. I needed to see the world," Amanda explained.

"I know," Alicia answered. "I knew you wouldn't stay. It was only a matter of time."

"You seem to have done okay for yourself, though. I see you're joining the convent," she stated, pointing up to her headdress.

"It's my calling. Just like New York was yours."

"Are you enjoying it?"

"Yeah, it's great. I've done my six months postulancy, and I'm partway through my two years as a novitiate, so, it's a fairly long process."

"As long as you're happy, then that's okay by me," Amanda answered with a grin.

"I knew you'd think it was strange. You never did like the nuns very much, did you?"

Amanda shook her head with a thin smile. Alicia was right about that. She found them to be incredibly infuriating and small-minded, but then, her life was just on a very different course than Alicia's was. The pair of them headed outside and walked around the grounds, talking, remembering their time together in the school growing up, and laughing. It was like nothing had changed, and yet, so much had. Amanda's life was so very different now and looking at her friend, she knew she would probably not see much of her after this. The world of the Magi was a dangerous one, and she did not want to expose Alicia to it.

Alicia took her to see the Mother Superior, who greeted her warmly and asked how she was. She always had a cordial relationship with Emmanuel, but they'd never been close. She'd been brought up by several nuns during her life, but she never really saw any of them as her mother. Some of them weren't incredibly affectionate, and Amanda often had the feeling that she was more of an annoyance than anything else. Although, that could have been her projecting her insecurities onto them.

Later, they sat in an empty classroom overlooking the central recreation area. It was break time, and the courtyard below was swarming with kids from the senior school. Alicia walked over and looked out the window that Amanda sat next to.

"Actually, you were always into that weird stuff, weren't you? Didn't the sisters catch you with an Ouija board once?"

Amanda smiled and nodded. "They did, yeah, that was grand. The looks on their faces were classic. Why do you ask?"

"I've got these four pupils in my class and they worry me. You can see them down there in the black clothing."

Amanda saw them right away. They were maybe seventeen or eighteen years old, which put them in the school's Sixth Form, so they didn't have to wear the uniform. There were rules about what they could and couldn't wear, but some kids were always pushing things. Amanda smiled. They were goths or emos, or whatever the term for them was these days. But they all wore black or dark coloured clothing and stood out from the crowd.

"The one with the long hair, he's Scott, his girlfriend is Christina," she said. Scott wore a black leather jacket and jeans with chains hanging from them, while Christina favoured a long black dress and an equally as long velvet coat, both of which complemented her white skin and black eyeliner.

Alicia continued to point out Tomo, who also wore a large leather jacket with clasps all over it, jeans, and huge jackboots, while the last of the four, Jake, was the least alternative of them, in just jeans and t-shirt.

"They're only goths, Alicia, nothing to worry about," she said.

"Maybe. But Jake used to be a straight-A student until he got caught up with them, and I've already caught them with a Ouija board, so…" She looked at Amanda and then away. "I know, I'm worrying over nothing."

Amanda agreed, she did think it was nothing, but to be safe, she used her Aetheric Sight and took a look at them in the Magical spectrum. There were no concentrations of Essentia around them at all, and they were certainly not Magi, who were usually easy to spot.

She looked back up to Alicia. "What do you want me to do?"

"They'll be in my class next, so they'll be busy. Take my skeleton key and just check out their rooms for me. You know what to look for better than I do."

Amanda smiled. It was somewhat ridiculous, but she wanted to be there for her friend, so she agreed.

It turned out she was right.

There was nothing in the rooms for Alicia to be worried about, Magical or otherwise. They were merely into some alternative culture and music. Out of the three of them, Christina seemed to be the one who was most into witchcraft, but it was all harmless stuff and had nothing to do with real Magic.

Amanda walked around the small dorm room, being careful not to disturb anything, and used her Aetheric Sight to give the room a sweep, just in case there was anything magical. But she saw nothing with any kind of Magical residue. Like the other rooms, Christina's was covered with posters of goth and heavy metal bands, as well as similarly themed film posters. A perennial favourite, *The Crow*, made an appearance in more than one of the dorms, with Brandon Lee staring out at Amanda with that brooding look of his.

Amanda sat on the bed and found herself filled with memories of her time here. She'd had a similar room to this one when she'd been here in the later years, and seeing Christina's room brought all those memories back.

As the end of Alicia's lesson drew near, Amanda made sure nothing had been moved and left the room, locking it behind her.

Amanda met Alicia later on in the reception area, sitting before the fireplace, which someone had now lit. The warmth of the flames was making Amanda feel very cosy, and she was looking forward to returning to the cottage soon.

"So, there's nothing for me to worry about?" Alicia asked.

"Nothing at all, but if you do find anything that concerns you, I mean, really concerns you, then please get in touch. You have my number; you can call anytime, okay?"

Alicia smiled. "Thank you. I know I worry too much, but I just want to help my pupils get the best start in life."

"I know," Amanda said. "And I know the kids won't see it, at least not yet, but they will understand it one day."

"I hope so, and don't you worry, I'll get a message to you if I discover anything that worries me," she said.

Amanda smiled. "Good. Now, I'm afraid I have to get going, but please do keep in touch, won't you?"

"I will," Alicia said.

With a warm smile, Amanda leaned in to give her friend a hug goodbye.

Alicia walked her out of the building and waved to her as Amanda set off along the driveway.

Part way along, once she was out of sight of the building, she turned into the trees and walked up into the woods. Coming to a stop, she looked around her. Feeling confident she was alone, she pulled on the threads of Essentia. She'd only Ported a few times by herself and she was still getting used to it, but even though it felt a little strange, it thrilled her even more.

Essentia surged, and with a snap of shifting air, she was gone.

- Diary of Ethel Peters, Howie's neighbour.

I got a good look at her today, and I'm sure it was the tramp from the stoop outside. It looks like Howard has taken her in. I noticed she was sleeping at the entrance to the building a few days ago. She always gave me a slightly scared look, but we can't have homeless people cluttering up the place, which was why I mentioned it at the last residents' association meeting. I think Howard was there that night as well. The chairman said he'd do something, but what can he do now that Howard's letting her live with him?

She's a pretty girl, lovely long red hair. She looks a lot better now that she's cleaned herself up a bit, but I don't like the idea of her living next door to me. I'll mention it to the chairman when I see him next. See if anything can be done.

Broken

London, England

Liz sat back with a sigh, leaning against the sofa allowing the blood to circulate back into her legs. She'd been sat on them for the past hour, going through any and all rituals they could find to try and tap into the magic that they believed the stone tablet held, but so far nothing had worked, and they'd just finished their final ritual.

"Well," said Fran, sitting beside Liz on the floor, "that's it. That's everything we know."

"Damn it, I felt sure something would work," Stephen exclaimed.

"It might not actually be magical, you know," Fran suggested.

"Sure, you might be right, but it's still disappointing. I was convinced there was something special about this thing."

"Well, if there is, it's a little beyond us, I think," Fran suggested. She turned to look at her sister. "You okay?"

Liz nodded. She was fine. She'd just been catching her breath and watching them try to figure out what they might have been doing wrong. Ben sat on her other side, also looking a little dejected and bored.

They were in the front room of Stephen's house while his parents were out for the day, which it made for the perfect opportunity to test a few of their theories on the tablet. This was the first time that Liz had really had a chance to look at it properly. The artifact had been kept in Stephen's house—in his Dad's office for safekeeping—and although she'd seen it a couple of times before, those had only been very brief encounters. Today, they'd all finally been able to get a good long look at it.

It was undoubtedly a mystical-looking thing, but there was a mundanity to it that had made Liz doubt just how magical it might be.

Lifting herself up, Liz sat on the sofa and enjoyed the comfort of the plush furnishing. She always liked coming to Stephen's house. His parents were well off, and they lived in a large, gated property in an affluent part of town. It made her kind of dread going home to their two-bedroom apartment with their mum. It wasn't like she could criticise their mother, though. Bringing up two girls on her own was tough. She worked hard at her two jobs to bring home the money to keep them going. The downside of that was that they hardly saw her, so they had to learn to be reasonably self-sufficient. These days, they usually washed their own clothes and made their own meals. They wanted to lighten the load for their mum as much as they could so that when she got home she didn't need to do much and could relax.

As Liz sat there, lost in her own little world, Ben got up off the floor and sat beside her. She turned and smiled at him and gave him a quick kiss. They'd just started dating, and it was still early days, but she was enjoying the ride nonetheless.

Fran had been pushing for her and Ben to get together for a while now, but Liz had felt nervous. She'd never had a boyfriend before and wasn't sure what to do or how it should go. Fran had shared her own experiences, of course. She'd already had several boyfriends and had been offering advice to Liz since she'd finally said yes to Ben.

"Well, that was a great big waste of time," Ben whispered to Liz, keeping his voice low so as not to be overheard by the other two.

"Not really. It just means we know what doesn't work. There's bound to be lots of other things we can try," she said with a smile. Ben, out of all of them, was the least interested in magical stuff. He went along with it and knew that it sometimes worked, but it seemed to make him nervous, like he was afraid of it. He was more interested in the latest Sci-Fi film or comic book, an interest he shared with Stephen, more than the girls. Liz had read a few of his comics now, though, and sat through a few films. She enjoyed them, but like her sister, she was more focused on the occult side of things.

"I suppose," Ben said, sitting back.

Liz smiled and shook her head slightly before looking up at Stephen and Fran. "So, do we have time for anything else?"

Stephen checked the clock. "Hmm, probably not. I think we should get packed up and then we can have a hunt online to see if we can find anything else out. I don't want my folks walking in on us doing this."

Everyone nodded. Stephen then set everyone to a job like putting stuff away, or taking some of the occult items and moving them back up to Stephen's room.

Liz finished her errands quickly and returned to the living room where Stephen was picking up the last few things, leaving only the stone slab on the floor. He looked over at Liz, then down at the tablet, and then back up at Liz.

"Do you think you can mov... No, actually, it's okay."

"Move the tablet back?" Liz asked.

"Well, yeah, but it's heavy. Are you sure you can manage it?"

"Sure," Liz said with a smile.

"Okay, I'll be back in a moment if you find it a struggle," he said and left the room. Liz reached down and started to lift it, only to find the thing was much heavier than she had thought it would be. She lowered herself down, got a better grip on it, and tried again. She couldn't help but gaze at it and marvel at some of the carvings—it was incredibly intricate.

She started to walk towards the study in the next room but quickly realised she didn't have the hold on it she thought she had. Shifting her hand, she attempted to get a better grip, only for one of the protuberances in the carvings to dig into her hand. She yelped as the artifact slipped from her hands and watched in horror as it dropped to the floor.

It felt like the world had suddenly slowed down as she watched it fall, twisting in the air as it went.

"Shit," she hissed.

With a bang that reverberated through the house, the tablet hit the floor flat. Liz stared down at it, her eyes wide with shock. There was a huge crack that ran right across the middle of the item, splitting it in two.

She'd broken it.

As she stared down, horror turned to regret, and tears welled up in her eyes, blurring her vision.

"What was that?" Stephen said, appearing at the living room door.

Liz looked up at him, feeling terrible. "I'm so sorry."

"You didn't," he asked.

"Yeah, I did…"

"You dropped it? Oh, God no. Where is it?"

Liz found she could only stand there and cringe as Stephen began to panic. She pointed down to the floor. A chair was hiding the mess from Stephen's view. She wanted nothing more than the earth to swallow her up and end her humiliation.

"How could you…Fucking hell, my Dad's going to kill me," he ranted.

"I'm sorry, it was a mistake," she said. "It was too heavy and it was digging into my hands," she tried to explain as she looked down at the palms of her hands. She could barely make out any details at all, though, through the tears streaming down her face.

Stephen moved up and looked down at the smashed artifact. "Damn it, it's really messed up," he said crouching over it.

Fran appeared at the door. "What happened?" she asked and stepped up to Liz, hugging her close when she saw the broken artifact. "It's okay."

"I couldn't hold it," Liz whimpered.

"That's alright, we'll figure it out. Are you hurt?"

"No, I'm okay," she said. "Stephen, I'm really sorry…" she said, but Stephen waved his hand and shushed her.

"Err…" Liz stammered, not sure what to make of his reaction. "What?"

"There's something here," Stephen stated.

"Where?" Fran asked.

"Inside the tablet, there's something hidden in there. Come here, have a look," he suggested, his voice full of wonder.

Frowning at the change of tone in Stephen's voice, Liz moved around and had a look down at the artifact as Stephen pulled on one end of the broken tablet. The top half slid away easily to reveal something metallic inside. It looked like it was made out of gold. A fresh wave of awe washed over Liz as she realized that whatever this was, had been entombed inside the tablet this whole time.

"Oh, my God," Fran said in amazement. "Liz, you found something."

"What is it?" Ben asked.

"I have no idea," Stephen said, taking hold of the golden item and pulling it. It slid out of the tablet smoothly. Moving it over to a nearby table, Stephen placed it down to get a better look at it. Liz eyed it as well and came to several conclusions right away. The first one being that it looked like a book. But a book made out of gold.

It looked like the main bulk of the object consisted of numerous golden pages, held together on one side by three golden rings that fed through holes on the sheets of metal.

Placed centrally on the cover was a large red gemstone. A ruby, maybe? Around it were intricately carved patterns and designs as well as several strange runes.

Stephen fingered the corner of the cover page and lifted it up.

"Careful," Fran whispered.

"Don't worry," Stephen said as he lifted the page. The action of the book was smooth and just as easy to open as turning the page of a paper book. Inside, each side of each page was divided into two columns and filled with text. There were clearly two different languages written here, and Liz wondered if this might be just two versions of the same text. The first language style was known as Cuneiform and was wedge-shaped, but she'd never seen the other one before. It was a sinuous swirling text, which had a kind of beauty to it.

As Stephen flicked through, it was clear that each page was basically the same layout, with no pictures or illustrations.

"This looks like it's worth a lot of money, dude," Ben whispered.

"What do we do with it?" Fran asked.

"I want to study it," Stephen answered her, still fascinated with the book. "I'll hide it from my parents; they don't need to know about it."

"What about the tablet?" Liz asked.

"Don't worry, I'll…" he paused, and looked back at the mess on the floor, and then looked over at the cat which was still curled up on a seat a short distance away. "We could make it look like the cat knocked it off or something," he said.

"Great idea," Fran said.

"I'll just hide the book first," Stephen said, closing it carefully.

"I'm really sorry, Stephen," Liz said as he picked up the golden book.

"Don't apologise. If you hadn't dropped it, we would never have found this. So, we're cool, okay?"

Liz smiled, feeling a little better.

- A passage from an unknown diary.

Poor Raven, he was beside himself today, knowing he was about to meet her. I think he finds it all a little too much. I know I find it confusing and I'm the one to blame!

Legacy

Paris, France

As the flash of light faded from her eyes, the noise and smells of the city assaulted Amanda's senses. They were stood in a back alleyway in Paris, surrounded by dirt and dumpsters filled with bin bags. The stench of rotting food was quite intense and a brief wave of nausea passed over her. She held it together though, and pinched her nose, looking around to make sure she wasn't getting dirty by brushing up against something. She wore a fitted grey turtleneck sweater, a short, pleated, black and white tartan skirt, tights, and tall, black-velvet boots, which so far had avoided the grime in the alleyway.

"What is it about Magi and alleyways?" she said, her voice sounding all nasally due to the grip she had on her nose. "We're always in them."

Gentle Water smiled at her but didn't answer.

She knew the answer to the question just as well as he did. They were a necessary evil when you wanted to Port around a city. You needed somewhere to appear that was out of sight.

"Are we close, GW?" Amanda asked.

"Yes, we are," Gentle Water answered. He used to frown when she shortened his name or used a nickname, but he seemed to be getting used to it.

He led the way along the alley, past more boxes and black bin bags filled with garbage, and stepped out onto the bustling

Parisian street. Cars honked their horns as they fought their way along, while cyclists weaved between the vehicles. People were everywhere, walking in every direction, going about their business.

Going from the calm environment of the Irish countryside to a busy urban street came with a certain amount of culture shock.

"Feck me, it's busy," she said, enjoying the view. The whole scene reminded Amanda of her time in New York, and part of her longed to return there sometime. Now that she was a Magus, she wanted to go back and not have to worry about how she would live. She wouldn't be fighting for scraps anymore. She could buy any house or apartment she liked and finally enjoy the city.

For now, she had other things to think about, though.

"There is Legacy House," Gentle Water said, pointing to a building across the street. The large three-story house was box-like, with a pitched roof and surrounded by a tall brick wall. This city wasn't like New York, the buildings only went up a few stories, so they didn't need to worry so much about privacy. As they approached, Amanda started to feel the Essentia that was at work here and looked at the scene with her Aetheric Sight. The building glowed brightly and was clearly well protected. Powerful Aegises enveloped the whole house and garden, and no doubt had an entire range of effects built-in. This was a well-protected coven house, which made sense given the status of the coven it was home to.

"Are they expecting us?" Amanda asked.

"Of course. They know we here already," he said.

"Really, you know that?"

"No Magus get this close to Legacy House without them knowing," he said.

"Of course, makes sense," Amanda mused to herself. She followed him across the street, keeping pace with her mentor as he led her up to a small door-sized metal gate. Without hesitating, Gentle Water reached for the latch and opened it without issue. Amanda could see the waves and ripples of Essentia cascading over him and then parting to allow him entry. Amanda followed and could feel the energy play over her, making the hairs on the back of her neck stand on end. Once again, the Essentia seemed to welcome her, allowing her to pass through the Aegises and into the garden.

On this side of the gate, the noise of the city faded to almost nothing, and the weather seemed more pleasant as well. The energy and kineticism of Paris fell away to be replaced with a calm peacefulness as they walked up the garden path.

The front door was wooden with big iron hinges and was painted a deep, strong blood-red. Looking up at the house, Amanda made out three floors above her, and the whole place almost pulsed with powerful Magic.

Amanda paused, feeling a little overwhelmed and slightly scared. Gentle Water stepped up beside her.

"Are you okay?"

Amanda smiled. "I am. I'm just a little, well, nervous, I suppose. I've only really met one Magus before."

"You met Inquisitor at airport," he corrected her.

"Yeah, okay, fair play to yeh, but I didn't know who he was, so that doesn't count."

"Everyone here friends, you be okay," he reassured her.

Amanda took a breath and pushed the nervous feeling away. She wanted to enjoy this moment. She'd learnt so much since becoming a Magus, but now she was taking her first steps into this world from her isolation in Ireland. She'd learnt the theory, now it was time for the practical lesson.

But despite learning so much, as she stood on that threshold, she knew she still had so much more to find out.

Amanda forced herself forward and stepped up to the door. She noticed that there was something metallic inlaid into the wood at about head height and took a closer look at it. Made from a lattice of steel, it was about the size of a football, circular, and in the shape of a serpent eating its own tail.

"Erm, what's that?" Amanda asked.

"That is ouroboros. It symbol meaning cyclicality, unity, or infinity. It also Legacy logo," he said.

"It's a bit ugly, is what it is," Amanda said, wrinkling her nose up at it. Disregarding it, she reached up and took hold of the metal ring that was held in the mouth of a metal lion's head on the door, and knocked.

The report from the knocker was loud and as she finished, she stepped back to wait. Moments later, the door opened and a rather handsome man stood in the entrance. He was tall with long black hair, a regal expression on his face, and a powerful nose. His swarthy skin had a roughness to it that suggested years out in the wilderness. He wore simple baggy combat trousers, boots, a vest top, and little else.

The man smiled right away, radiating warmth. "Gentle Water, whassup, *Chebon*? How you doing?"

"I am well, Raven. It too long since I see you," her mentor answered.

"Too right, it has," he smiled and looked over at Amanda. "And you must be Amanda?"

She smiled. She liked him already. He clearly worked out. The muscles on his arms were well defined, and he had a lean look to him, like a coiled spring ready to leap into action. "Nice to meet you," she said, offering her hand.

Raven took it and lifted it to his mouth. He kissed her hand with a smile. "The pleasure is all mine, Miss Page," he answered, his gaze lingering on her for a moment. Then he let her go and stepped back. "Come in, come in, you must be eager to see the place, Amanda. I bet Gentle Water has been telling you all about it."

Amanda smiled at the subtle dig at Gentle Water's usual laconic nature. He often didn't speak much, preferring to keep quiet when talking wasn't needed.

"He's told me a bit, yes, but I am keen to have a look around," she said.

"Then, by all means, go, have a look. I'm sure Gentle Water can show you the place. And when you've finished, come back to Royston's office. He'd like to meet you too."

Amanda nodded. She'd heard of Royston. He was the Legacy's current coven leader, something which rotated every few years.

Raven left them to it, so Amanda turned back to Gentle Water and smiled. "He's nice." Gentle Water had told her of some of the people she was likely to meet at the Legacy House, including Royston, Raven, and others. As far as she was aware, Raven was a few hundred years old and had grown up as a Native American back when they were known as Red Indians by the frontiersmen of the old west. She hoped she'd see him again today.

"Shall we look around house?" he asked.

Amanda smiled, nodded, and followed her mentor's lead into the room to the left of the door they came in. They found themselves in a large, well-appointed living space. It looked like some lavish mansion with wooden Art Nouveau chairs and tables, amazing oil paintings in gilded frames adorned the walls, and polished, delicate-looking ornaments stood regally on top of side tables. Amanda spotted a fish tank off to her right and wandered over. She came to an abrupt stop a short distance from it as she noticed there was a miniature blue whale in it, breaching, and then splashing back down.

"What?" Amanda said to herself in wonderment. She got closer and saw dolphins and sharks and all manner of sea creatures in there, swimming back and forth. "Jaysus, this is fecking crazy," she muttered.

"Magic," Gentle Water said from close by.

"Is there more stuff like that in here?" she asked.

"Lots more."

They moved across the room and into another even larger chamber at the end of this one. Again, Amanda paused, and looked back the way she'd come, and then out the windows, checking what she saw until she felt sure she was right. She looked over at Gentle Water.

"It's bigger on the inside, isn't it?"

Her mentor smiled. "Well done."

Amanda shook her head and kept walking, marvelling at the fantastic room around her. As they entered the next one, she spotted someone sitting on one of the seats. It was a woman, at least a few years older than Amanda, with long, wavy brown hair. She looked up and smiled. Amanda was about to smile back and walk over when a dark shape slipped past her feet.

"Excuse me, young lady," the cat said.

"Oh, I'm sorry…" Amanda replied and moved out of the way, only to stop and think about what had just happened.

She looked over to Gentle Water. "Did the cat just speak to me?"

"Yes," he answered.

"Oh, good, as long as I'm not imagining things."

"Don't worry, that was just Merlin," said the lady in the room who was approaching them now. She wore a long, flowing, brightly-patterned dress and a charming smile. "I'm Maria," she said and embraced Amanda gently, placing a kiss on her cheek. "You must be Amanda, Gentle Water's new apprentice we've heard about."

Amanda smiled back. "That's right."

"And how are you finding it? This house, I mean. It's your first time here, right?"

Amanda nodded. "It's amazing, there's so much to see."

"I'm glad you like it," she said and then turned to Gentle Water. "The boys are in the kitchen, you might want to introduce her to them."

"Of course," Gentle Water said. "Shall we?"

Amanda nodded and said farewell to Maria as they walked over to a door on the right. Passing through a few more rooms, they soon reached a room at the back of the house. As they approached, Amanda could hear a group of men talking.

"Unfortunately, I don't think there will be any female gargoyles at the party," said a deep male voice with an American accent. "Maybe I can find you a rock with a hole in it," he continued, laughing.

"Cute. I'll be running security there, though, and have no desire to watch you try to seduce some poor unsuspecting girl," replied the deepest and roughest voice Amanda had ever heard. It didn't even sound human, more like two huge boulders grinding together.

"Seduce? Hah! That's a joke, Xain's idea of a chat-up line is, 'do you want to sit on my lap and see what pops up?'" said a man with a softer American accent.

"Says 'Mr Come-Look-At-My-Guns,'" said the first voice.

"Jeez, I'm going to faint from all the testosterone in here," said a fourth voice, this one was more nasally with a British accent.

"Getting all light-headed around us real men, Loomis? Don't worry, your balls will drop one day," replied the first voice.

Laughter broke out as Amanda followed Gentle Water into the room. She couldn't get a clear view of the men at first, but as they spotted Gentle Water, a cheer went up.

"Hey, it's my main man."

"You're back already?"

"Welcome back."

Amanda stepped out from behind him and smiled at the three men ahead of her. Wondering where the fourth was, she turned and for a moment she thought she saw Horlack, the Scion who attacked her in the alleyway, standing there in the kitchen.

Her reaction was immediate, as terror shot through her, and she stumbled back into the countertop, grabbing it to steady herself.

The thing moved, looking surprised, and as she got a second look at it, she realised it wasn't Horlack at all, but it was a Scion. A huge one that looked like it was carved from stone with a leonine face and two huge, bat-like wings sprouting from its back.

"Holy Feck," Amanda exclaimed as adrenaline shot through her body, making her heart rate skyrocket. Gentle Water and the others leapt to her aid.

"Are you okay?" Gentle Water asked.

"Whoa there. It's only Balor, he won't hurt you," said a broad-shouldered black man with tattoos up his neck and close-cropped hair. He was the one with the strong American accent.

"Are you okay?" the other American asked, sporting a long black trench coat and short dark hair.

"I'm sorry," Amanda said. "I just wasn't expecting…" she cut herself off and pointed up at the Scion. "Scared the bejaysus out of me, so yeh did."

"She attacked by Scion werewolf during Epiphany," Gentle Water explained. "This first time she see Scion after that."

"I'm sorry," the Scion said.

"No," Amanda said. "It's not your fault, please, don't apologise. I need to get used to these things," she insisted, standing to her full height. Taking a breath, Amanda composed herself, stepped forward, and offered her hand to the hulking form before her. "Hi, I'm Amanda."

The Scion hesitated for a moment before it reached forward, gently took her hand in its massive claw, and tenderly shook it. "Call me Balor," it rumbled.

"Balor. Sorry for the reaction just then, I just wasn't expecting to see something like you in the kitchen."

"Understandable," Balor answered. "No need to apologise."

"May I break up this love in and say hi? I'm Xain," said the large black man. He shook her hand with vigour.

From the other side of the kitchen, the Caucasian man in the trench coat waved. "Orion," he said, introducing himself.

"Loomis," said the final man in his British accent. He was the skinniest of the three and wore glasses, had wild hair, and sported a long, grey coat.

"Don't sound too happy about it," Xain said to Loomis. "She'll die of boredom just standing there."

"Lovely to meet you all," Amanda said, smiling warmly at them as her thundering heart slowed.

"Are you sure it's lovely? I mean, come on, look at Loomis here, I'm not sure lovely is the right word," Xain said.

"Oh, my God, you're so funny. Oh, shit, there goes a kidney," Loomis said sarcastically.

"Heh, well, you're some of the first Magi I've met since Gentle Water found me."

"He told you to lower your expectations, right?" Orion said.

"Well, honestly, I had no idea what to expect." She liked these guys. Their smiles and easy banter endeared them to her right away. She felt like she could hang out with them and have some fun times.

"She's disappointed," Xain said, winking at her and then turning to his friends. "I blame you," he said to Loomis.

"These men do many dangerous missions for Legacy," Gentle Water explained.

"We get to do the fun stuff," Xain cut in excitedly.

"Yeah, you're a regular James Bond," Loomis commented and then turned to Amanda. "He's modest too, if you hadn't noticed."

Amanda smiled back. "There's nothing wrong with being confident."

"Oh, I like you already," Xain stated, grinning from ear to ear as he stepped up next to her and put his arm around her shoulders.

"Oh, bloody hell, now you've gone and done it," Loomis said. "His head will never fit through the door after this."

"We'll never hear the end of this," Orion groaned.

"Want to join the team?" Xain asked her, letting go of her shoulders. "I sense a vacancy is about to open up."

"Not today," Gentle Water cut in. "We go see Royston now."

"Ah, well, you'd best not keep the boss man waiting," Xain answered.

Amanda walked through the kitchen behind her mentor towards the opposite door. "I'll catch you all later, guys," she said.

"See ya."

"Laters."

"Goodbye, Amanda," Balor said.

"Call me," Xain said, making a telephone gesture with his hand.

Amanda smirked as she left the room. She'd be sure to find these guys again soon.

Eventually, she followed her mentor into a library. It was a large two-story affair with racks of books lining the walls and some comfortable looking leather seats in the middle of the wood floor. Sitting in one of those chairs was another woman Amanda hadn't seen before. She rose from her chair at seeing Gentle Water and Amanda walk in, and with a courteous smile, walked over.

She was a slim beauty in a long, black dress that hugged her curvy frame. Her long, raven-black hair fell in perfectly controlled waves, surrounding a pale face with deep red lips. Her dusky eyes had a fierce quality to them that suggested a predator, but Amanda felt no threat from her.

"Aaah, Maya, nice to see you," Gentle Water said.

"Bonjour, Gentle Water," Maya said. Even though she used the French for hello, her accent was soft and cultured, suggesting that Maya had spent plenty of time abroad to mellow her underlying French accent. "And this must be Amanda," she said, offering her hand. Amanda took it, and Maya air-kissed her beside each cheek. "We have heard so much about you, mademoiselle."

"It's lovely to meet you, too. This is an impressive library you have here," Amanda said, marvelling at the endless rows of books.

"Thank you. The coven has been collecting them for centuries now. There's not a lot of fiction, but there's plenty of other volumes here to keep you occupied."

"I'll look forward to having a look, so I will."

"Have you been showing Amanda around?" Maya asked.

"Yes," Gentle Water answered.

"We met Xain, Orion, Loomis, and Balor in the kitchen," Amanda said.

"And you're still here? Glad they didn't scare you off," Maya joked.

Amanda smiled. It seemed like this woman, who projected an air of calm detachment, had a keen sense of humour, too. There was something about her, though, that felt somewhat familiar as if they knew each other, but Amanda was reasonably sure she'd never met Maya before.

"We go see Royston next," Gentle Water said.

"Well, don't let me hold you up. Royston is a busy man, I'm sure he'll be waiting for you," Maya said.

"Lovely to meet you," Amanda said, smiling, and they left the library behind, making their way back around to the front entrance and down through the middle of the building to a closed door. Gentle Water knocked, and a man invited them in.

The office was well appointed with a large ornate oak desk that dominated the far side of the room, with several chairs in front of it and a seating area to Amanda's left as she walked in. She recognised Raven standing to the left of the desk, while an older man with grey receding hair in a shirt and trousers stood behind it as they entered.

"Amanda, finally, welcome to the Legacy, it's such a pleasure to meet you. How are you finding it so far?" Royston asked as he walked around to greet her, offering his hand. Amanda grasped it, and he placed his other hand on the back of hers as he gently shook it with a smile.

"It's been great, everyone has been very friendly. I had a bit of shock when I first saw Balor, but everything was okay."

"I'm glad. Yes, Balor can be a scary sight, but he's a gentle giant to us Arcadians. We have a room ready for you upstairs, which we'll show you later. But tell me, how's your training going?" he asked as he walked back around his desk.

"It's been grand to be sure, thank you," Amanda answered. "Gentle Water has been a wonderful mentor. He says I've reached the rank of Knight," she said with a smile.

"Knight? Already?" Royston asked in surprise, looking at Gentle Water.

"She fast learner," Gentle Water said.

"You're not kidding. Well, you *are* doing great, then," he said, indicating that Amanda should sit down.

"Thank you," Amanda replied, feeling a slight flush of embarrassment as she lowered herself into one of the seats opposite Royston.

"So, correct me if I'm wrong, but you have already encountered a Scion, other than Balor, I mean?"

"Yes, I was attacked in New York by one who Gentle Water called Horlack."

"Indeed. He's been missing for hundreds of years, but his legend is well known amongst the Magi."

"And then in the airport, I had to fight off an Inquisitor," she said.

"I've heard reports of this. You've had a lucky escape, young lady. Not many Magi would survive an Inquisitor attack so soon after their Epiphany. You clearly know how to look after yourself."

"Heh, well, it's no bother," Amanda blushed, feeling embarrassed by the compliment. "I've had some self-defence training, so I have. You don't survive the streets of New York if you can't look after yourself."

"Well, I was about to send Raven here off on a routine mission to London. It seems that a Nomad we're aware of has been sniffing around some of the Magic shops over there, and we thought we'd check it out. Would you like to join him? I'm sure Gentle Water can sort your room out for you while you're away."

Amanda raised her eyebrows in slight surprise and smiled. A mission, so soon? she thought. And she got to spend time with Raven, who she really rather liked the look of. She looked over at Gentle Water. "May I?"

"You not need my permission, Amanda. You capable Magus, make own choices."

Amanda looked back at Royston. "Then, yes, I would love to." She grinned, feeling a rush of excitement in her chest. Finally, after all her time training, she was actually doing what she had silently promised to Georgina after realizing she could have healed her. She was acting. She was doing something.

"Excellent, then it's settled. Raven, you may leave at your leisure," Royston said.

"Um, can I ask, is the ball still happening tonight?" Amanda asked.

"It is, indeed," Royston said. "8pm at the Musée d'Orsay; we'll be Porting over there from here."

Amanda turned to look at Gentle Water. "I haven't had a chance to get a dress," she said. "Will I have time?"

"I suspect so," Royston said.

"Leave it with me," Gentle Water said.

Amanda smiled. "Oh, okay, sure."

"Amanda," Raven cut in, looking at her. "Are you ready?"

"I am," she said, rising from her seat.

"Then let's not waste any time," Raven suggested and offered her his hand.

Stepping forward, Amanda took his hand in hers, feeling the sudden build-up of Essentia around him. The air snapped, and they were suddenly in another backstreet, but the feel of the city was different again.

Following Raven out of the alleyway, Amanda guessed she was in the heart of London, England—her Magical insight mentally pinpointing her location and confirming her suspicion.

Amanda felt the Magic flare around Raven, and a Link request from him blossomed in her mind. She accepted it.

~Thanks,~ Raven said through the Link.

~No bother,~ Amanda answered without speaking. ~So, what's the plan?~

~We're going to visit some magic shops and try to figure out what the Nomad is doing. They've been spotted in a few of them now. Mainly, the few reputable ones that also deal in real Magical Artifacts.~

~What, like Vorpal Swords plus one?~ Amanda asked grinning.

~Something like that,~ Raven answered. ~I didn't peg you as a gamer.~

~When you're raised in an orphanage where role-playing games are banned, you just know the kids are going to find a way to play them, right?~

~Heh, I suppose so. Well, there are many Magical items out there, some more powerful than others, and there's a thriving black market that trades in them, mainly run by independent Riven and the small organisations they create. Some of the world's magic shops pick these items up and sell them on. As a result, some of the shopkeepers know a thing or two about real Magic, which makes them a valuable and accessible resource for anyone wanting some advice.~

~So, is this Nomad after information, or are they hunting someone who is?~

~Maybe we'll find that out today,~ Raven said.

They walked along the streets of Soho, along small, single-vehicle-wide roads that crisscrossed this part of the city until Amanda spotted a shop in the corner of a bend that proclaimed itself to be The Magician's Hat.

"Follow me," Raven said.

"Is this a real Magic shop?" Amanda asked. "I mean, does a Magi run it?"

"No, Mr Travers is not a Magus, but he is an Initiated Riven, so he knows what to look for. He's a useful informant to have."

"Sure," Amanda said, as she suddenly noticed a small flare of Magic from within the shop. "What the…"

Raven froze in his tracks and put a hand out to stop Amanda too, as the door to the shop opened and four teenagers ran out of the building. Led by a blonde-haired youth, Amanda noticed right away that there was a strong concentration of Essentia coming from them, but it was proving difficult to pinpoint it. She could feel it, she knew it was there, but she couldn't see it. They were on the opposite side of the street as Amanda watched them run by, only to notice another flare of Essentia from within the shop and then simultaneously another flash a little way in front of the gang coming from a side street.

A woman with long blonde hair stepped out of that side street, right in front of the kids. Amanda's Magical sight picked up the obvious glow of concentrated Essentia coming from her that marked her as a Magus. The kids came to a sudden stop, looking terrified while the blonde woman stared at them, her expression smug as a smile spread over her face.

"Angel," Raven muttered quietly and started to stride over to her. Amanda followed.

Amanda noticed Essentia stir around Angel, and the lead boy suddenly grabbed his throat. He seemed to be struggling to breathe.

"Hey," Raven called out as Angel drew closer to the four kids. Angel looked up with a startled expression, clearly surprised to see Raven and Amanda. The four teenagers looked around, too, obviously scared half to death.

As they crossed the street, Angel's look of surprise vanished and changed back to the cruel smile she had worn moments earlier as her Magic faded and the blonde-haired boy caught his breath again.

~Get those kids to run, wait for my distraction, then throw up an Aegis around us, including Angel, got it?~ Raven sent through their Link.

~Got it,~ Amanda answered.

"Raven, why, what brings you here?" Angel asked, her soft voice light and casual.

Keeping behind Raven, Amanda waved to the four kids to get their attention, before silently urging them to run with a sweep of her hand.

"Legacy business," Raven said, his tone professional and detached. "We heard you'd been snooping around the place."

Angel smiled. "Keeping a lookout for me, have you?"

Essentia flared from within Raven, and a simultaneous surge grew around Angel.

Amanda took that as her cue, and called on her own Magic, throwing up the Aegis around them all.

Angel's Essentia hit the inside of the Aegis, but the shield held as more Magic flared around the Nomad.

Raven's Aegis sparked in her Magical sight as Angel blasted him with Essentia, but his shield held firm.

"What are you trying to achieve?" Angel asked, backing up, away from Raven as he approached her. Amanda kept behind him, pumping more Essentia into the big Aegis that kept Angel here.

~Are they gone yet?~ Raven asked her through their Link.

Amanda glanced back up the street in time to see the kids duck down a side alley. Angel would find them within moments if they let her go now. ~They need a minute or two more,~ Amanda answered.

"Anything that frustrates any plan of yours, is a win for me," Raven said, never taking his eyes off Angel.

Keeping his distance from her, Kinetic energy surged out of him and threw Angel against the wall. She hit it with a crunch.

"Wow, Raven, I never knew you could be so forceful," Angel purred, smiling.

"Get your mind out of the gutter," Raven ordered. "What were you after those kids for?"

"Oh, you know, the usual," Angel said, while her Magic continued to slam against Amanda's containment Aegis. Amanda kept flooding the Aegis with Essentia, repairing the damage that

Angel was inflicting, but it wouldn't last forever. Angel was a skilled Magus and would break through soon.

"Really?" Raven answered suspiciously.

"So, what are you going to do, kill me in the street?" Angel asked.

Amanda looked up the road. There were a few people around, but they hadn't really noticed the confrontation going on. They couldn't see the Magic that they were using. To the average Riven, it just looked like they were having a tense conversation.

"Don't tempt me, Nomad," Raven said.

"But, Raven dear, you know how I feel about a little temptation," she said, breathing in and making her chest strain against her shirt. It was already unbuttoned low enough to show off her cleavage.

"Fucking Nomads," Raven sighed.

Angel's Essentia continued to hammer Amanda's Aegis. She could feel it faltering.

~I can't keep her contained much longer,~ Amanda sent through their shared Link as she watched Raven's Magic fight against Angel's.

~Don't worry, I think those kids are in the clear,~ Raven answered, as Angel's Magic slammed into her Aegis again, and smashed a hole clean through.

Essentia flared once more, and Angel Ported away, disappearing from view. Amanda glanced up the road, but no one was watching.

She cancelled her Magic and checked the street around her, wondering if the Nomad might suddenly come at them from another direction, but she seemed to be gone.

"What the hell was all that about?" she asked, turning to Raven.

"No idea, let's go ask Mr Travers, shall we?"

"Sure," Amanda answered, and followed Raven up the street, looking around suspiciously.

Today had been a day for new introductions, meeting the members of the Legacy and now her first Nomad. She remembered being in the Dark Side nightclub, hanging out with Howie's friends as he worked his shift. She'd often visit and soon got to know the other security guards and bar staff, she also got to talking to some of the regulars.

Stuart was one of those regulars. A quiet man who said he used to be a boxer but was now working some tedious job somewhere. He lived alone and wanted to do something more suited to his talents as a former boxer and street fighter.

Another of those she'd befriended, after complimenting her on her fabulous shoes, was Georgina. She came to the club early most nights and had a drink or two before leaving. After they'd swapped pleasantries following Amanda's shoe compliment, they'd seen each other most nights.

Georgina was friendly but seemed kind of troubled. Amanda had no idea why, even after they'd hung out outside of the Dark Side, Georgina was still something of a closed book. Despite this, they soon became good friends, hanging out regularly and enjoying each other's company.

Then, one evening, a man Amanda had never seen before walked in and started to drag Georgina forcibly out of the club.

Amanda had protested but was no match for the larger man, who pushed her away and continued to hurt Georgina, only for Stuart, in his typical no-nonsense manner, to walk up and knock him out in a single punch.

The police arrived and knew the man right away. He was a well-known pimp, and they took him in for questioning.

Amanda sat with Georgina afterwards and expressed her horror at what had happened. "I wonder why he was after you?" Amanda asked.

"Oh, Amanda, have you not figured it out yet?" Georgina asked.

"No," Amanda answered.

"I'm a prostitute, Mandy," she'd said. "He was my pimp."

After becoming what she had thought was quite close to Georgina, and counting her as one of her friends, this revelation came as something of a shock. Georgina had been kind about it, though, apologising to her several times. She'd not really known the slang that Georgina had been using and had made some false assumptions. She remembered feeling shocked, but after a while, once she was over the surprise, she'd been more curious than anything else.

Stuart had been amazing. Strangely enough, the reason he'd stepped in was not only because he was basically a nice guy, but it turned out he was also one of Georgina's john's and wanted to protect her from her pimp.

After that, Stuart offered to protect her full-time and from that day forward he was her pimp, although, he was very different from many of the others out there.

Looking back now and remembering Stuart stepping up and saving Georgina, she wondered if her subconscious Magic had anything to do with it.

It was only a little over a month later when Howie broke some bad news to her.

Having her living with him and not contributing to the groceries and bills was putting a strain on him and he could no longer provide for both of them going forward. In other words, Amanda had to get a job, something that wouldn't be easy given she was in the country illegally. Howie seemed like he wanted to help, but at the time his comments about her not contributing had only pushed Amanda away. She felt like he was distancing himself from her, when in fact, it had probably been her own self-doubt and her feelings of inferiority that had made her retreat.

She told Georgina, her only other real friend at the time, who sympathised. Amanda was here illegally, and Georgina was doing an illegal job, so it seemed only right for her to talk to Georgina about it rather than Howie. Georgina even started to give Amanda money, just a little bit here and there so she could give something back to Howie, but it wasn't enough.

Sitting in the Dark Side one evening as Georgina handed Amanda another stack of bills, Amanda found herself looking at it and considering where it had come from.

"Here, take it, Mandy. I've got to hit the streets. We'll catch up later, okay?" Georgina said, standing up from her seat.

"What's it like?"

"Sorry?" Georgina asked.

"Doing what you do. You know, what's it like?"

"Why? I've told you about it before, how come you…" she said, when sudden realisation passed over her face. "No, Amanda, that's not a good idea, you shouldn't…"

"You do it," Amanda cut in.

"Well, yes, but I wouldn't recommend it."

"I'm sure sewer workers wouldn't recommend their job, either. I'm asking you, though. I need the money. I can't keep taking it from you. It's not enough anyway. I need to start helping Howie out, so I do."

Georgina sat back down. "Amanda, this is not a good thing to do. It fucks you up if you're not careful. It exposes you to drugs and worse. If the police catch you…"

"If the police catch up with me, I'm going to be deported anyway. What's the difference? You've got Stuart now, though, and I know you've quit the crack again with his help."

"Well, yes, I have," she sighed. "Look, I can't stop you. If you want to work the streets, you can come with me and I'll show you how to do it, but I want to be clear, I don't think this is a good idea for you."

"I understand. I think I know what I'm letting myself in for."

"Do you? Because I'm not so sure."

"I've heard your stories many times now. I'll be fine."

"Have you ever actually had sex before?"

"That's irrelevant," Amanda blushed.

"You're a virgin, aren't you? Shit, Amanda, this is not a good idea."

"I'm doing it," Amanda said, feeling more resolute than before. She was convinced she'd be fine. She felt like she knew what she had to do, and she felt sure she could defend herself, too. Howie had been teaching her some self-defence techniques these last few months since she'd been living with him.

Georgina stared at her for a long moment and Amanda stared back, determination etched across her face.

"Okay, fine. When do you want to start?" Georgina said.

"Tonight," Amanda answered.

"Of course you do."

Later that night, in the early hours, she stood in the shower, cleaning the grime and smells off her body, scrubbing herself down, washing away the taint. She cried, not quite believing the new low she had sunk to. But the next morning, seeing Howie smile as he thanked her for the rent money, washed those feelings away. Suddenly, she knew why she was doing it and she didn't care what it was she'd done the night before to get it.

As the days and then weeks passed, she learned to deal with it, to cope with the feelings that the routine stirred up. It was a means to an end, and the money was good.

She was quite aware that her situation was unique, though, and that nearly all the other working girls were in a very different position. Eventually though, the inevitable happened and Howie found out. She never discovered how, but his feelings were clear on it, and he threw her out.

She wished she'd found another way, some other job that would allow her to keep living with him, but it was too late by then. She couldn't give up the money and even if she did, Howie wasn't likely to let her move back in.

As she thought back to her choices and experiences, she could see her latent Magical skill guiding her, helping her, and making the best of her life choices. Her Magical luck wouldn't turn her into a billionaire overnight, but it would affect her life in lots of small ways.

As Raven led her into the magic shop, the bell above the door ringing as they passed through, Amanda scanned the interior space while Raven walked over to the counter. She spotted a few Magical items, glowing softly with their concentrated Essentia. It seemed that the Magician's Hat really did serve the Magical community.

Following Raven up to the register, she looked up to see a man who looked to be in his fifties. He was greeting Raven in the manner of a friend, his lined face smiling and radiating warmth.

"And who have you got with you today?" Mr Travers asked.

She offered her hand. "Amanda. Nice to meet you."

He took her hand and greeted her. "So, what brings you here today?"

"Those four children and the blonde woman who were in here moments ago, do you know who they are?" Raven asked.

"I've seen the blonde woman in here a few times recently, but I've never really spoken with her. The kids have been coming here for a while, though. I think the blonde one is called Stephen, but that's all I know."

"Did they talk to you today?"

"Yes, they wanted me to translate something. I didn't get a chance, though, because the woman spooked them and they ran from the shop. I looked back and the woman was gone, too. Freakiest thing I ever did see."

"And the text, did you see it?"

"Briefly. It was cuneiform, if I remember rightly."

Raven continued to question him, but there was little else to learn.

After a short while, the pair of them stepped outside and onto the grey London street.

"So, what's the craic, then?" Amanda asked.

"You sensed the Essentia coming from those kids, right?" Raven asked.

"To be sure. Difficult not to. I couldn't get a clear view of it, though."

"Neither could I. The kids themselves weren't Magical, so I'm guessing they had something on them, maybe in that one's backpack."

"The blonde one? Probably. You think that woman was after it, too?"

"Angel? Yes, that's exactly what I'm thinking. She's a powerful one, you need to be careful of her. But if Angel is hunting whatever it is those teenagers have, then it must be worth her time and effort."

"To be sure. So, those kids have something powerful, then?"

"Powerful and dangerous. I bet they have no idea of the shit they're in. We need to find them before they get themselves killed."

- London, England.

Angel stood in the penthouse hotel suite she'd taken for her stay in London and looked out over the rooftops of the lower buildings around her. She'd been cursing silently to herself since her little confrontation with those accursed Legacy Magi. It wasn't the first time she'd encountered Raven, but she wasn't sure who the redhead was.

She was pretty and had a surprisingly strong ability with Magic. If circumstances were different, she'd be interested in her in other ways, but she was apparently a Legacy Magus, which condemned her as far as she was concerned.

She'd had those kids in the palm of her hand. They were right there, and whatever the artifact was that they had on them. But now they were gone. She wanted to rip those two Arcadians apart for meddling in her affairs.

Anyway, she couldn't dwell on this, she needed to find those kids, and right now her best chance was the informant she had in Yasmin's coven, Xander.

With a thought, she sent a pulse along her Link to Cherub. It opened up quickly.

~Yes, my Baal?~ Cherub said in Angel's head.

~Send a message to Xander through the usual channels, get him to contact me directly,~ she said.

~Of course,~ Cherub answered, and closed the link.

She'd find those kids and take that artifact from their cold dead hands, and if she saw that redhead again, she'd take great pleasure in killing her, too.

Blood Bath

London, England

"You couldn't breathe?" Liz asked, her hackles rising as Stephen described the feeling he'd had when they'd encountered the woman on the street.

"Not at all. My lungs just stopped working. I couldn't suck any air in. It was really strange."

"And scary, I bet," Fran said.

"Very," Stephen answered.

"I would've had your back, dog," Ben cut in, his tone defiant.

"I know, matey," Stephen said, smiling. "Next time we'll be ready for her."

"You bet," Ben said.

Liz gripped Ben's hand tighter and smiled to herself. He sounded brave, but she knew he was just as scared as the rest of them had been back there. He'd never admit it, but Liz knew him well enough now to know that he was all bravado.

"Any idea who those two people were who saved us?" Liz asked.

"Saved us?" Ben questioned her.

"You know what I mean," Liz said, rolling her eyes at Ben. He probably didn't like the idea that she thought they were out of their depth, but she felt reasonably sure that Ben and Stephen hadn't felt or saw what she and Fran had.

On their way out of town, she and Fran had used a public washroom. Fran had asked Liz if she'd seen the glowing swirls of light that had been coming from the blonde woman and had felt the rush of energy. In hushed tones, Liz had told her sister that she had seen it. They wondered what it meant, but guessed that they'd just witnessed some real-life Magic. They couldn't be sure, of course, but it was the only logical explanation.

"Yeah, I know, babe," Ben replied and winked at her.

"No, I've no idea who they were," Stephen answered her. "But it looked like the blonde knew them."

"They didn't look like they were friends," Fran commented.

"No, they didn't. But they helped us get out of there," Liz added, choosing her words carefully.

"Think we'll meet them again?" Ben asked.

"No idea," Stephen answered. "Do you think they were after the book?"

"That would be my guess," Fran replied.

"And mine," Liz joined in.

"Well, those fuckers can't have it," Ben said defiantly.

"Damn right," Stephen joined in.

Liz rolled her eyes again but kept quiet. Boys and their macho bullshit, she thought. They were approaching Stephen's house in north London, walking the last few meters up the street and taking their time about it. She knew, like they all did, that once they were there, they'd each head back home, but only once the book was safely back inside Stephen's house.

They turned into the driveway and walked up to the front door, where Stephen paused. She looked up, unsure of what was going on.

"What's the problem?" Fran asked. "Oh…"

"What's the matter?" Her sister sounded concerned, which got Liz's attention. Stepping forward, she looked past Stephen to find the door to the house standing ajar.

"Mate…" Ben started to say.

Stephen stepped inside, calling for his mum.

"Just hold on a second… mate!" Ben called after him. Fran followed him inside, right on Stephen's heels. Liz hesitated for a moment and then ran in after her sister with Ben close behind her.

It was dark inside the house and there was a rancid smell hanging in the air. Liz followed Fran into the front room, peering into the shadows. Stephen and Fran had stopped just inside the door. The smell was much worse in here. Liz crossed the threshold and craned her neck to look over her sister's shoulder, right into a vision of Hell.

The walls were awash with dark red bloodstains. Around the room, in the comfortable chairs and on the sofa were several bodies that had been eviscerated. Liz recognised them all.

Liz clamped a hand to her mouth as her eyes came to rest on the body of her mother, sitting alone in a chair, her torso ripped open all the way up from her crotch to her collarbone. Her insides had spilt out into her lap, and her ribcage was clearly visible amidst the gore.

She was dead, but her eyes were wide open as if in surprise.

Liz felt bile rise up from her stomach as she noted the corpses of Ben's and Stephen's parents. They'd been cut up too.

For a couple of seconds, no one said anything. Was it a dream? A nightmare? Surely, this couldn't be real. She'd wake up in a second and all would be well. Stephen's parents would greet them all warmly like they always did and this horror would be forgotten. But that didn't happen.

Liz's body convulsed involuntarily. She wanted to throw up.

Movement further into the room caught her attention, and a figure stepped out of the shadows. He was about six feet tall, wearing only a blood-stained vest and loose cargo trousers with sturdy boots. His whole body, apart from his hands, face, and neck was covered in tattoos. In any other situation, she'd have considered him a handsome man with his chiselled features and short blonde hair, not to mention his well-muscled physique. But the massive knife in his right hand and the blood that covered him from head to toe showed him in an altogether more sinister light.

"Welcome friends, you're just in time. I've been waiting for you. As you can see, I got a little bored and had some fun, but now that you're here, the real fun can begin," he said with an American accent.

"What... What the... Oh, God, this can't... Who are you? What the hell is this? What have you done?" Stephen asked, incredulous.

"Whoa, slow down. That's too many questions, young man. I think introductions are in order, don't you? So, I'm Nate," he said. His tone was light, conversational almost. It was alien-sounding in this setting. Why was he being so friendly with this massacre all around him? "Now, come on, don't be shy," he said, almost laughing. "It's only proper that we introduce ourselves.

Beside Liz, Fran pulled back and grabbed her arm, urging her and Stephen to move as Nate advanced on them. "Come on, we gotta go," Fran whispered.

"But… I don't… Mommy? Daddy?" Stephen said, his voice sounding small and cracking with emotion. Liz had never heard him call his parents by those labels. It was probably the shock.

"Stephen, move. Come on, Liz. Ben, move back, Ben," she hissed at him.

Ben shoved his way past them, rage distorting his features. "Go! Get them out of here," he called back to Fran.

"No," Liz called. "Don't! Come back."

"Get out of here!" he yelled at her.

His shout in her face shocked her and made her back up and follow Fran out.

"Oh, how gallant," she heard Nate say as Fran bodily pushed her and Stephen out the house.

"We have to leave," Fran ordered them.

"What about Ben?" Liz asked.

"He'll follow, come on," she answered as she dragged them both down the driveway.

The front window exploded outwards as something heavy was thrown through it. Liz looked back and saw Ben hit the ground.

"Ben!" she yelled, making a dash back the way she'd come.

Nate suddenly appeared out of thin air with a *thwip* noise, standing over Ben. Liz jumped back in shock, along with Fran and Stephen.

"Wait," Ben croaked, looking up at Nate and pushing himself up onto his hands. Nate only smiled, lifting the huge dagger into the air behind him and slashed down at Ben with it.

Blood whipped out from Ben's neck and splattered Liz's top and sprayed across her face.

As she watched, Ben's head rolled back as his neck, nearly severed, gaped open. Blood poured out from the fatal wound, his arteries squirting. It was still attached by a sliver of viscera, though, and hung there for a moment until Ben's arms gave way, and he dropped back to the ground.

"No!" Liz screamed as desperation and hate washed over her. Fran and Stephen grabbed her and pulled her back. "Let me go!" Liz shouted. She didn't care about Nate, she didn't care if she died, she only wanted to save Ben, even though she knew it was too late.

Fran grabbed her, took her face in both of her hands, and forced Liz to look at her. "Liz, he's dead. We have to go, now, or we die, too," she said, her voice commanding and fierce.

Liz glanced sideways and saw Nate look up with a wild grin and eyes alight with excitement of the impending hunt. Liz looked back at her sister and nodded. She had no idea what to do. She wanted to help Ben, but he was gone now. She knew it, even if she didn't want to believe it. But Fran was taking charge, and Liz was more than happy to follow.

With her sister holding her hand, Liz ran. They sprinted out into the street just as two large black 4x4s barrelled towards them. One of them mounted the curb and skidded to a stop in front of them. The other skidded to a halt behind them, closer to the house.

Men in black jumped out, carrying large guns and... swords?

What was going on?

More men jumped out of the vehicle. One of them wore a long, tan trench coat and looked at Liz and her friends.

"Get in the car, now. We have to leave," he said.

Liz followed her sister and Stephen and doing as they were told, they climbed into the back of the car. She could already hear gunfire coming from Stephen's front garden.

The all-terrain-vehicle wheel-spun and turned one hundred and eighty degrees before accelerating down the road in the direction it had come from.

"Are you okay?" the man in the passenger seat asked.

"What the hell's going on?" Fran asked.

"I'm here to help you. That was a Warlock, and he would have killed you," he answered, his tone flat.

"He killed our parents," Liz whimpered, the reality of which she was still struggling with.

"I'm not surprised," the man replied. "Look, I'll get you to safety. My men will deal with that one, but others will follow."

"Who are you?" Stephen asked.

"I'm Vito, we're part of a group who fight these Warlocks and protect the innocent. Trust me, you're safer with us."

- An internal message within the Black Knights Coven

Baal Yasmin,

I have just heard from Nate that he feels this is all taking a little too long to come to fruition. He sounds quite frustrated by all the waiting around for the Inquisitor to make his move. I fear he may take matters into his own hands. This may actually help us, but I felt the need to inform you of your apprentice's state of mind.

Yours for Eternity,

Kez

Ball

Paris, France

Amanda stepped out of the bathroom, having had a refreshing shower, and rubbed at her hair with a towel, trying to dry it. She walked around into the main bedroom and marvelled at the spacious suite that was all hers. She had a living space with a small kitchenette, a large bedroom with a grand four-poster bed, and en-suite bathroom. Everything was elegant mahogany wood panelling, paintings, and mirrors with ornate gilded frames, porcelain lamps, and brocade flocked wallpaper. She wandered over to her bed and admired the pretty white Cheongsam dress that Gentle Water had given her after returning from London.

It was a long, fitted white dress with a slit up one leg made in the Chinese style. She ran her fingers over the silk, enjoying its softness and admiring the pretty pattern.

"What time is it?" she asked herself. She instantly knew the exact time the moment she said it as her Magical senses kicked in.

"It is nearly seven o'clock in the evening," said a voice in her room.

Amanda ducked back in shock and covered her nakedness with the towel. "Who's there?" she asked, looking all around. She couldn't see anyone. Everything glowed with magic as well, so that wasn't much help.

"Sorry to scare you. I'm only here to help," said the voice, which sounded male to Amanda.

"Where are you?" Amanda asked.

"Over here, on the wall," it said.

"On the wall?" Amanda stepped forward, still clutching the towel in front of her. "Where? Near the mirror?" She guessed it was something Magical. She'd already had a conversation with the cat, so it was probably something like that again.

"I am the mirror," the voice said.

Amanda looked up and spotted a small face carved into the golden frame at the top of the mirror. As she peered at it, it moved and smiled at her.

"Oh, feck," she exclaimed. "You're alive?"

"Greetings. Kind of. I'm only a mirror, gifted with a modicum of intelligence by the Magi of this esteemed establishment, and I'm here to help," it said in a jovial tone.

"And you've been here this whole time?"

"I've been here for hundreds of years, ma'am. But I stay quiet unless I am needed."

"Can you see me?"

"But of course," it smiled back, blinking its eyes.

"Aaah," Amanda grimaced. She'd been getting changed in here and had walked through the room naked at least once before as she'd prepared for her shower.

"I understand your concern. But I am just a mirror, and not gifted with belonging to one or the other gender. I have no interest in you beyond wanting to help you whenever I can," it explained.

"Oh. Well, that's okay, then, I suppose," Amanda said, relaxing. "I was just wondering how close we were to going to the ball tonight."

"I believe it is about to start," it said.

She'd been looking forward to this ever since she'd heard about it. She wondered what kind of affair it would be. Would she meet more Magi or maybe some celebrities? Raven had mentioned it was some kind of fundraiser or something. She wasn't sure what that meant, but if there was going to be some drink and nice food, she was happy.

Walking back to her bed, she placed the towel down and pulled some of her favourite underwear out from the chest of drawers and started to get dressed.

Before she'd met Georgina, she'd never really taken much interest in clothing. She'd always just worn what the nuns had given her, which, looking back, had been some of the most boring and frumpy clothes she had ever worn. She didn't have the money to go and buy anything of her own, although she did steal a few bits from lost and found, or modify some of the clothing she'd been given. She'd either rip bits off her skirts to make them shorter or intentionally wear them wrong, like the tie that was part of her school uniform.

She didn't care and often chose not to bother tying her shoelaces because she knew it would annoy the sisters.

Once in New York and living on the streets, her only interest in clothes was that they were warm. Once Howie had taken her in, he'd bought a few bits for her, and while there was the odd thing she liked, and his intentions were honourable, most of the stuff he got for her just didn't appeal.

Eventually, she met Georgina and struck up her closest friendship since Alicia. It wasn't long into that friendship before Georgina took her on the first of several shopping trips to some of the discount clothing stores and bought her some stuff. Previous to that, everything she'd had was either practical or modest, often both, but Georgina had other ideas in mind.

She picked out everything from sneakers to high heels, fitted jeans to elegant dresses, and some of the prettiest underwear she had ever seen. Putting it on for the first time, Amanda felt like a new person. Howie could barely speak when she walked back into his apartment in her new outfit.

He later admitted that he thought she liked the long skirts and loose jumpers she owned. Now, she was skipping about in mini-skirts, camisole tops, and ripped jeans. Pretty much the total opposite of what she'd been forced to wear at the orphanage.

She smiled at the memory. She'd been such a frump before New York.

Getting dressed, she eventually pulled on the dress before checking out her reflection

"What do you think?" Amanda asked the mirror, feeling like she was in some kind of fairy tale.

"You'll be the belle of the ball," it said.

"Charmer," Amanda answered, before picking up her clutch bag and leaving her room.

She met up with Royston and Gentle Water in the vestibule. The two men smiled at her as she walked down the stairs towards them.

"Wow, you look stunning, Amanda," Royston said.

"Thank you, you look good, too," she said, admiring his sleek tuxedo.

"Ready?" Gentle Water asked.

"Where's everyone else?" she asked.

"Most are already there. There are a few more to follow as well, but it's better we go over in small groups, less conspicuous," Royston said.

Moments later, Gentle Water had Ported them all into a back room of the museum and was leading her out into the main hall.

The building was a vast converted train station with a huge arched roof of glass. An ornate gold clock sat at the far end, looking over the main hall with its statues and paintings. People were everywhere, talking or admiring the art, while waiters weaved between them offering drinks and canapés.

Everyone looked gorgeous, wearing long cocktail dresses or sharp evening suits. Amanda picked up a glass of champagne from a passing waiter and smiled at Gentle Water. "God love yeh, this is amazing."

"You welcome," he said, sipping his own drink.

"I'm going to get a better look, so I am," she said and walked over to the edge of the balcony. As she watched the people move about, she picked out a few famous faces amongst them, including some Hollywood movie stars she recognised.

As she enjoyed the scene below, Amanda became aware of someone approaching.

"Hi there," Maria greeted her softly, sliding in beside her and getting quite close. Amanda felt Maria's hand caress her hip, and shifted her weight, turning slightly to pull herself away and put a little extra space between them.

Amanda smiled. "How are yeh? I didn't see you there." She could feel the heat in her cheeks.

"What do you think?" Maria asked, looking out over the museum below.

"It's impressive. I've never been anywhere like this before."

"Never?"

"No, I, er... I led a fairly sheltered upbringing, so I did. I had a TV in my room when the sisters thought I was old enough, but I've never been to a museum before."

"That's a shame," Maria said, looking over the top of her glass from beneath her chocolate hair. Her soft pink lips smiling.

Maria was standing quite close still, Amanda thought, but she didn't mind and smiled back.

"I'd be happy to show you some more of the world if you like," Maria offered.

"Yeah, sure, that sounds great. I'd love to experience new things like this," she answered, looking over the museum again. She looked back. Maria was closer still.

"You enjoy new experiences, then?" Maria asked.

"Yeah, sure, I guess," Amanda said, unsure where Maria was going with this, and then she felt Maria's fingers, tracing lines over her hip.

"That's a very healthy attitude, Mandy. I wish more people were open to such things, don't you?"

"Heh," Amanda blushed, both enjoying it and feeling a little uncomfortable about Maria touching her. "Yeah, I suppose," she said as Maria shifted closer and slipped her hand around her waist. "Oh, um, careful," Amanda said, moving her glass out from between them.

Maria looked her up and down with her sultry gaze, drinking her in. Amanda felt like she was under a microscope, being studied and observed. She smiled at Maria, and for just a moment, she let her do it—she let Maria touch her and actually kind of enjoyed the feeling. She felt the warmth and thrill of arousal burn deep within her, and for a split second, she wanted to pull Maria in, kiss her, and explore the curves of her body.

She remembered one night back in New York when Georgina got a call from her old escort agency. They had a former client come back asking for her and gave her a call. It happened occasionally. Amanda had been working the streets for a while by then after being kicked out by Howie. She had her own tiny apartment in the same block as Georgina, where they often hung out together, preferring each other's company to being alone.

Georgina had ended the call and turned to face her. She'd just finished a slice of Georgina's divine baked vanilla cheesecake. That desert was to die for.

"You're not busy tonight, right?" Georgina had asked.

"I'm not, I have a night off," she answered, licking the fork clean.

"I have a job offer if you're interested."

"Oh, go on," Amanda urged.

"That was my old escort place, they had a client call asking after me," she explained.

"You want me to take it for you?" Amanda asked.

"No, no. He wants a threesome, him and two girls."

"Oh…" Amanda answered, feeling uneasy.

"So, we'd have to put on a bit of a display for him, you know, cos he likes that…"

"You mean, you and me, we'd have to…"

"Have sex. Yes, Amanda, we'd have to fuck," she said bluntly.

"Um, thank you for thinking of me, but I don't think I swing that way, you know?"

Georgina smiled. "Heh. That's okay. We're friends, so I thought I'd ask."

"Why did you think I would be cool with that?"

"It's only sex, Mandy. You do it with strangers most days, so what's the difference?"

She thought about it for a moment. Georgina was right, but this was different. It wasn't the action that made her stomach go tight with anxiety. It was the possibility that she might ruin her friendship with Georgina. She didn't think it was worth it. Or maybe it went even deeper than that, she thought. Maybe the sisters had really done a number on her head. Was there a hint of Catholic guilt eating at her subconscious? Did she think it was wrong? She shook her head, hoping to dislodge that troubling thought. No. It just wasn't worth her friendship with Georgina, that's all. And yet…

But Georgina accepted her rebuttal, and called another friend. She went out and did the job with someone else, and Amanda spent the whole night thinking about what it would have been like if she had done it. If she were honest with herself, part of her was kind of excited by the idea, but it scared her as well. It took a huge mental leap to admit to herself that the idea of being with a woman was kind of exciting. It was taboo, but that was what made it interesting.

She ended up eating another slice of Georgina's heavenly cheesecake while she was out, just to try to take her mind off of the idea of sex with Georgina.

It didn't work, but was a tasty distraction while it lasted.

When Georgina eventually returned, Amanda asked her how it went.

"I thought you weren't interested," Georgina teased.

"I, well… Um… I'm not, to be sure… But, you know," she said, swallowing guiltily.

Georgina raised her eyebrows. "You are interested, aren't you?"

"No! No, I'm not. I just wanted to make sure you had a good night, you know?"

Georgina smiled. "Of course. Oh, helped yourself to more of my cake, I see?"

Pushing the memory to the back of her mind, Amanda took a breath. She felt like she was stood on a fence, ready to fall either way, and unsure which way to lean. She could feel Maria's gentle warmth, and looking up, knew she could lose herself in those deep brown eyes. She was tempted. So very tempted.

Amanda reached around to Maria's hand and lifted it off her hip. She stepped back a touch and smiled. "I'm flattered, I am, but I'm not…. you know…," she stammered, unsure how to voice it. "At least, not right now."

Maria smiled back. "Of course, I'm sorry, I thought I was getting signals from you. You can't blame me for trying, can you?"

"I don't mind, no. I like you, Maria. Sorry," she answered, wondering if she really had been giving off signals. Maybe? She had been admiring Maria from a distance a little bit. She kind of fascinated Amanda, although she wasn't sure why. Or was she not willing to admit it to herself?

"I hope I've not offended you," Maria asked, concern crossing her face.

"No, don't worry, you haven't. We're fine."

"Good. I'm sorry."

"To be sure. No harm done," Amanda answered, her tone conciliatory.

Maria smiled. "So, are you looking for some fun and frolics tonight?"

"Not really. I've had a crazy few days, so I just wanted to have a drink and chill out a bit."

"Of course, I heard that you met your first Nomad today with Raven."

"Yep, some woman called Angel, I think. She wasn't much trouble," Amanda mused.

"Well, there were two of you against her, and in a public place, as well. Don't underestimate her. Angel is a well-known and dangerous Nomad."

"I won't." Amanda wasn't worried. Angel hadn't put up much of a fight, so she was feeling pretty confident.

The night went on, and Amanda circulated through the people she knew, speaking with Gentle Water, Raven, Maria, and Royston. Maya was there, but they didn't talk much.

"Is Maya okay? She seems quiet," Amanda said to Royston partway through the night as she looked over at the brooding figure standing at the balcony.

Royston looked over. "She's fine. She likes to keep to herself. She has her own stuff to deal with."

"Her own stuff?" Amanda asked. "Does she have her own coven or something?"

"Oh, okay, I'm guessing no one told you. She's a Scion. A vampire, to be precise," he said.

"She's a vampire? You mean, she drinks blood?"

"That's part of it, yes."

"So there are two Scions in the Legacy Coven? Her and Balor?"

"Correct. Some are more involved with the Magi than others. They have their own society and internal politics to deal with. But we don't get too involved with that. Most Scions don't associate with us much, and those who do, don't usually mix with their own kind."

"Good to know," Amanda said, looking back over at Maya, who was still standing at the balcony, looking out over the sea of people below. She looked lonely, but also clearly didn't need or want company, either.

A little later, Amanda decided to explore the Museum. The place was huge, and many of the side rooms were deserted or had just one or two other people in them.

She was admiring a painting in one of the side rooms when someone spoke to her from behind.

"And you must be Amanda," said the dusky female voice.

Turning, Amanda looked up into a face she had not seen before. The woman had a long black mane of hair, shot through the purple streaks. It framed her angular face as she stood there in an elegant, glittery-black mermaid dress. Amanda could also feel the Essentia that was leaking off of her. She didn't need to open her Aetheric Sight to know this woman was a Magus, and probably a powerful one.

Amanda smiled and offered her hand. "To be sure, and you are?"

The woman took Amanda's hand gently in hers and gave a slight smile. It was as if she had just had something confirmed to her, something that made her happy. The woman didn't answer right away, and Amanda was just starting to wonder if she might need to ask for her name again when the woman seemed to rise from her internal thoughts.

"Yasmin," she answered.

"Charmed." Amanda smiled.

"Are you here with your Legacy friends?" Yasmin asked.

"I am. They're over that way, you could go and say hi," Amanda offered.

"I'll pass, thank you. I just wanted to introduce myself as I had heard of your arrival," Yasmin explained. "I'm sure we will cross paths again soon."

"It seems like everyone knows who I am," Amanda mused out loud. "But I have no idea who's who here."

"Probably best that way, there could be some unsavoury individuals within these walls," Yasmin answered with a knowing smile.

"Perhaps. Are you sure you won't come over and say hello? Go on, they're a friendly bunch, so they are," Amanda urged her.

"Maybe another time." Yasmin smiled. "I'll see you around, Amanda." As Yasmin sashayed away, Amanda couldn't help but admire her and the way she glided over the polished floor. She was a stunning and yet dangerous beauty.

- A passage from Royston's diary

I got a message today. She's called a meeting. It seems the time has come. Here we go…

Escape

London, England

Liz, along with her friends, walked up the centre of the church, ushered along from behind by Vito. The church priest was beside this intense man, who had saved them from the killer at Stephen's house. Everything felt a little unreal as if she were dreaming. She wondered if she might wake up suddenly, back in her own bed, cosy and warm. But every time she closed her eyes, she saw flashes of her mum, dead in that chair, or Ben, his head tilting back, his neck gaping wide as blood spilt everywhere.

"Yes, yes, I got the message. You can use my office in the back. What's this all about?" the priest asked.

"Vatican business, sorry, it's on a need-to-know only basis. We just need the use of your church for a night," Vito explained.

So, Vito was from the Vatican. Was he a priest? Liz wondered.

"I mean, okay, sure, it's yours, but wouldn't a hotel be better?"

"No," Vito answered, refusing to elaborate further.

Liz and her friends were shown into an office at the back of the church, behind the altar. It was a small room with a humble desk covered in various papers. Hymnbooks stood in stacks on the floor, while a wardrobe stood ajar revealing the robes the priest wore for mass and other events.

Vito grabbed three chairs from around the room and placed them in the middle of the office. "Sit," he barked. It was an order rather than a request.

They sat down, herself on one end beside Fran, and Stephen on the other end.

She held her sister's hand, gripping it tightly as emotions and images of death filled her mind.

"So, tell me what happened tonight," Vito said once they were settled. Liz looked up at him. He seemed a little annoyed or accusatory, and Liz started to take a dislike to him. When he'd rescued them, she hadn't really looked at him in great detail; all she knew was that he'd saved their lives, and for that, she was grateful. But now that they were away from the immediate danger, and she actually had calmed down enough to assess him on his own, her opinion of him was starting to drop.

He seemed to have an agenda here, but she wasn't sure what it was yet. Liz didn't want to speak to him and kept quiet. Luckily, her sister was apparently feeling a little more vocal.

"We nearly got killed by a madman. You were there, you rescued us," she answered, sounding a touch annoyed by the question.

"Yeah, thanks for that," Stephen added. "But what about our parents? Should we go to the police? He killed our friend…" Stephen looked away, his voice cracking with emotion before he could finish.

Hearing him get emotional caused Liz's breath to catch in her own throat as she thought about Ben. She thought about the thug who killed him with a smile on his face. Cut his head off. The sight of the open wound on Ben's neck flashed into her mind again. She felt sick, but somehow held it together.

"Ben Marshal, yes. But what interests me more is why the Warlock killed him."

"What?" Fran asked.

"Why did that Warlock kill your parents and friend? What was he after?"

Liz's mind went immediately to the one thing they had with them that might be of interest to a Warlock like Nate. The golden book was still in Stephen's bag. Did Vito know it was there?

"No idea," Fran answered, her tone defiant. "This is ridiculous. All this talk of Warlocks is crazy. We should go to the police and report him for God's sake."

Vito moved quickly, stepping forward he swung his hand around in a powerful slap that caught Fran full on the cheek. The sound of his palm hitting her filled the room. She yelled. The force of the hit was so strong that she was knocked sideways, away from Liz and into Stephen. He fell. Fran fell, and their chairs were knocked out from under them.

Liz gripped the seat of her chair with her hands, rooted to the spot.

"Hey, there's no need for…" the priest called out.

"Shut up, Father. And you…" Vito spat, looking to Fran, "don't take the Lord's name in vain, Witch." He drew out that last word, filling his voice with as much hate and bile as he could muster.

Liz watched Stephen roll and get up, anger glinting like cold steel in his eyes, but Vito had seen it coming and reached for something under his jacket. He withdrew a gun and pointed it at Stephen before he could move in.

Stephen froze and raised his hands. "Hey, chill out, let's discuss this rationally."

Liz looked down to see Fran on the floor, pushing herself up, but staring at Liz, her eyes wide.

Liz mouthed the word, "What?" silently, while Vito's attention was on Stephen.

With her eyes, Fran looked at Vito and then back at Liz, and then did it again. Vito was standing right in front of her but was staring at Stephen, his gun pointing at her friend's head.

Liz looked back at Fran, who silently formed the word, "Now."

Liz took a breath as she pulled her foot back and glanced up at the priest, who was opposite her on the other side of Vito. He'd seen the silent communication between her and her sister, and nodded to her, urging her on. With all the force she could muster, Liz kicked out. As she attacked, the priest lunged for the gun.

Her foot connected with Vito's closest leg just below the knee. He yelped as the priest grabbed the gun and raised it up, away from Stephen. It discharged once, its report echoing around the room and deafening Liz for a moment.

Vito fell to the floor as the priest prised the gun from him and then trained it on the Inquisitor.

Liz still sat in the chair, fear gripping her and keeping her rooted to the spot. She watched Stephen help Fran up as she rubbed the bright red slap mark on her cheek.

"Are you okay?" Fran asked.

"I'm fine," Liz answered.

"You guys best go, I'll keep him here," the priest said.

"Thank you, Father," Stephen said.

"No thanks required. I had no idea we let people like this into the ranks of the church. I will have some choice letters to send to the Vatican after today," the priest said. "Now, go, before his friends get here. There's a backdoor through there."

Stephen nodded and turned to his friends. "Let's go."

Fran grabbed Liz by the hand and led her out. Liz didn't resist, she just followed, feeling ever more bewildered by the day's events. Within moments, they were out the back and walking up a service road behind the church.

"What do we do now?" Fran asked.

"I don't know," Stephen answered, hiking his backpack further up his shoulder, the weight of the book inside giving him comfort. "Do you think he was after the book?"

"I don't see what else he would be interested in," Fran stated as they rushed up the road approaching a T-junction.

"Who are these people?" Stephen asked.

"I don't know, and I don't want to find out. So, which way?" Fran asked, looking left and right. Busy London streets awaited them at either end of the road.

"We should go to the police," Liz cut in.

"Is that a good idea?" Stephen asked. "They'll take the book."

"Forget the damn book," Fran barked. "I think we need to get help. We can't fight these people off. They've already killed Ben. Do you want to get us killed, too?"

"No, but can we just think about this for a minute?" Stephen asked.

"Ugh, sure. Which way?"

"Let's go right," he suggested and set off up the road. They had walked just shy of ten meters when a figure stepped out of the shadows and started to approach them. Liz stopped at the same time as her friends as they all peered into the darkness. As the figure approached the light, they finally got a good look at her. It was the blonde woman from the magic shop. She smiled as she approached them.

Liz felt her stomach drop. Was there no escaping them?

Liz remembered this woman's sudden appearance in the Magic shop when they'd gone to show Mr Travers the text they'd copied from the book. He'd looked at the script with interest, but before they'd really discussed it, the blonde woman was standing right behind them looking over their shoulders at the papers.

"How curious," she'd said.

Her sudden appearance had shocked everyone, including Mr Travers. Stephen had grabbed the papers from the shopkeeper's hand and led the sprint from the shop into the street. When the woman had suddenly appeared from a side street, the fear that had bloomed in her chest in the shop multiplied several times over.

But that fear couldn't stop other, stranger and equally worrying thoughts she'd felt on seeing the blonde properly in the street for the first time.

She'd never say this out loud, but frankly, the woman was gorgeous. Liz had no interest in women beyond seeing them as friends. She was only interested in boys, but there was something different about this woman. Something beguiling about her that overrode her usual feelings and stirred something deep within her. She wondered if Fran had felt the same. She knew that Stephen had been captivated by this beauty, that went pretty much without saying, but these feelings were alien to her.

She'd been at a loss to explain them, then. And now, as the woman swanned up the road towards them, her hips swaying as she shifted her weight from leg to leg, that same longing and arousal flooded back, creating a yearning and a need inside her that she was both captivated and disgusted by.

"Who are you?" Fran asked as they backed away.

Good thinking, Liz thought, keep her talking and distracted. If only she'd thought of that, but her mind was elsewhere.

"My darlings, why did you run away from me earlier? I only wished to talk to you," she purred.

Her clothing was a walking cliché, Liz thought. The sexy secretary look was so out of date and out of touch with what the world was like now, she thought. And yet, there was still something about this woman that made Liz want to ravish her and to feel those stocking-clad legs wrapping around her.

Those thoughts and feelings hadn't overridden her sense of survival, though. While she might be inexplicably attracted to her, she was also getting a strong impression from this blonde that she was a threat. She was dangerous, and she should be avoided. That was the only reason she was not running up to her and begging her to take her right then and there on the street. Instead, she continued backing away, confusion and conflict filling her mind.

"Talk? You just wanted to talk?" Fran asked.

Liz looked sideways. Stephen looked like he was in a daze. Fran was pulling him back, away from the blonde. Fran seemed the least affected by this angelic woman.

"But of course, unless, you wanted something more?" the blonde asked.

Liz felt her heart melt and the warmth of arousal build. *Shit, if she keeps talking like that, I'll orgasm just standing here listening to her.*

A strange feeling, like a gentle gust of wind, except there was none, flowed into her from behind, and she felt compelled to turn around. Someone was there, she knew it, and as she looked back at the blonde woman, Liz noticed she'd stopped walking too and was looking behind them.

Liz turned and saw Nate, the killer of her mum and boyfriend, stalking up the street from the opposite direction, trapping them.

"Angel, thank you for holding them here for me, I do appreciate it. Yasmin sends her regards." He still held that wicked bent knife in his hand.

Liz looked back at Angel, whose whole expression had changed from jovial and light just a moment ago to deadly serious. Nate had spoken to her in a friendly manner, and yet, Liz could sense intense hostility between these two.

She was no longer interested in Liz and her friends and Liz noticed that she'd suddenly lost the feeling of attraction and arousal towards Angel. It was like night and day, as if someone had just flicked a switch. She glanced down at Angel's body, which moments ago, she'd wanted to kiss all over, and now only saw another woman, someone she really wasn't interested in.

"Go, run, now," Angel said.

"What?" Stephen asked. He also looked like he'd been snapped out of some kind of trance.

"Run. I'll find you later. I need to deal with this idiot," Angel said as she stepped past them towards Nate.

Liz didn't need telling twice, and neither did her companions. She ran, breaking into a sprint as they raced out of the service road into the crowds on the London's streets.

Her heart was pounding and adrenaline was pumping. It felt like Nate would leap out of an alleyway or side street and attack them at any moment. She had no idea how long they'd been running for, but eventually, they stopped and caught their breath.

"You know what?" Stephen said, looking up at them. "I've changed my mind, let's go to the police."

- Notes from a police report

These children have been exposed to horrific events over the last few hours, and I recommend a full psychological evaluation to help them recover from what they've seen.

Experts from the Natural History Museum will be here in the morning to take a look at the artifact the boy brought in.

We're returning it to their room for the time being as its removal seems to have agitated all three of them.

Dig

Sahara Desert, Egypt

Amanda steadied herself as her boots sank into the soft sand atop the dune they had appeared on. The wind whipped about her as she looked around, making her skirt and scarlet hair flap about wildly. The first thing she noticed was the oppressive heat. It felt like she'd stepped into an oven.

"Wow, it's hot here," she said.

"Not if you don't want," Gentle Water answered her. Amanda smiled at him. He was referring to the fact that she could alter the temperature around her to suit her tastes if she wanted. He was right, she could.

"It's okay, I don't mind the heat," she replied pulling off the sweater she had on, leaving her in just a thin camisole and short skirt.

They were standing at the crest of a dune, overlooking the remains of a campsite that lay half-buried in the shifting sands. Nearby, a rocky plateau rose out of the desert a few hundred metres away, and Amanda had a strange feeling that something wasn't quite right over there.

She frowned and used her Aetheric Sight. Around the rocky outcrop, there was a colossal sphere where no Essentia floated in the air.

"Jaysus, what the feck is this shite?" she muttered to herself.

"Dead Magic Zone," Gentle Water said. "Magic not work there."

"Oh, well, that's banjaxed," she said to herself. Gentle Water was already making his way down the side of the dune into the camp, walking parallel to the Dead Magic Zone. "At least, we're not heading in there."

"We go in there, soon," he called back to her.

"Feck," she muttered as she half-walked, half-slid down the slope, sand pouring into the tops of her tall boots. "So, why are we here again?"

"This where Horlack was found before he attack you in New York. Royston think important for you to know," he said.

"Oh, they found him here? Look at this place, it's a right mess. No one's been here for ages."

Gentle Water nodded but didn't answer her as they walked into the camp. The tents were in disarray. They were either half-covered in sand or falling apart, their canvases ripped from the sand and left to flap in the wind. Some of the ones over to the right were almost entirely overcome by the encroaching dunes.

There were camping stoves, cooking utensils, clothes, tools, and personal effects scattered everywhere. Even a jeep fitted with wide tyres for use in the desert had been left here to be eaten by the Sahara.

"Where are the people?" Amanda asked as she followed Gentle Water around the camp.

"Dead. Horlack kill them. They were hired by Nomad hunting for artifact. Magic artifact. They not know who they work for."

"They were working for the Nomads?"

"One Nomad. Yasmin."

"Yasmin?" Amanda said, remembering the woman she'd met at the ball last night. "Shite."

Gentle Water turned to look at her, his expression asking the question for him.

Amanda sighed. "I met a Magus at the ball. She called herself Yasmin. Too much of a coincidence, right?"

"Right," Gentle Water replied with a frown and continued walking.

"I had no idea. She found me when I was exploring the museum. I didn't know who she was. I met so many Magi that night, I didn't think anything of it." Amanda explained.

"It okay. No harm done. You alive."

"I guess," Amanda said, feeling annoyed with herself that she hadn't spotted a Nomad when she'd had the chance. But then, that was probably why they were so dangerous. They could hide in plain sight.

When they'd reached the edge of the camp, Gentle Water paused to look up at the Dead Magic Zone before continuing towards it.

"Are these places dangerous?" she asked, eyeing the zone as it rose up before them while they approached the edge of the plateau.

"It not kill, there still Essentia there, but less, and Magic not work," he answered.

Amanda pressed her lips together in a grimace. That hadn't really eased her fears. As they grew closer, the feeling of wrongness, of something missing or out of place swelled in her chest until they walked through the outer edge of the zone and onto the plateau.

For a moment, it felt like Amanda couldn't breathe. Her enhanced senses, her connection to reality and the Essentia were severed, and she suddenly felt incredibly vulnerable. Had this been how it had felt before she'd become a Magus? She couldn't remember feeling this weak as a kid growing up in Ireland nor during her time on the streets of New York, and yet, this must have been how it was.

It was strange just how comfortable she'd become with Magic that the moment it was taken away she felt utterly defenceless. Walking on the rocks with her block-heeled boots was much easier than wading through the sand. It might be an uneven surface, but at least she wasn't sinking anymore.

Amanda stopped, sat down on a rock, and pulled off her boots, emptying the sand out that had built up inside them. Putting them back on, she jogged to catch up with her mentor, finally reaching him when he crested the side of the rocky incline and reached the relatively flat top.

Out of pure curiosity, she attempted to work some Magic as she walked, but nothing worked. It was as if she was no longer a Magus. The feeling was very disconcerting.

They continued walking and found more equipment, much of it smashed to bits and scattered over a wide area. The largest concentration of tools were sitting outside a large hole in the plateau that had been cut into the rock. It angled down into darkness on a gentle slope.

"We're going in there?" Amanda asked.

"Yes."

"Grand," Amanda replied with a hint of sarcasm. "Lead the way."

Gentle Water pulled a torch out of his pocket and started down the passage. Amanda followed, her boots echoing as they moved into the darkness. As they descended, the temperature dropped until Amanda decided to pull her sweater back on. The passage levelled off and a short distance further on, they entered a room. Cables ran down from the surface to work lights and other bits of equipment, none of which was working anymore. Some stuff down here had also been smashed up.

Gentle Water scanned each room, but he seemed to know where he was going. It was as if he were giving Amanda a quick tour of the place.

As they continued on, Amanda noticed a rather disgusting smell that grew stronger the further they went. By the fourth chamber, it was overpowering and it took all of Amanda's willpower not to start retching. She was holding the front of her sweater over her nose and mouth just to keep going.

Having never been in an Egyptian tomb before, she found the whole thing fascinating. If it hadn't been for the smell, she could've easily spent hours down here looking over the hieroglyphs that covered the walls. In the fifth chamber, Gentle Water walked over to a hole in the wall and turned to her.

Amanda stopped and looked up at him, sensing he wanted to show her something.

"Amanda. This where powerful artifact found. Legacy is following Yasmin and Inquisition, they hunting artifact through Cairo and London. Maybe Angel hunting it, too. We don't know."

"She seemed really interested in the kids we saw running from the shop," Amanda speculated, her voice muffled by her jumper.

"Maybe kids have artifact."

"Maybe…" Amanda mused, thinking it through. It was certainly possible. "Does the Legacy always track the Nomads and Inquisition?"

"Yes. Legacy, Council, and many other houses try to monitor Nomads, it is difficult. It constant fight."

"So, this dig was sponsored by Yasmin, who was probably looking for the artifact that was in here? So, how come she didn't get it? What happened?"

Gentle Water nodded. "Follow me," he urged and turned to head deeper into the crypt. Beyond the fifth chamber was a small anteroom with a large doorway into the next room. The massive stone slab that had been blocking it had fallen out into the antechamber. Gentle Water shone his torch down to make sure Amanda didn't trip as she stepped up onto it. As she did so, she saw traces of blood on the slab and a few small shiny things that looked like slightly bloody plastic, about half an inch long. She crouched down to get a better look, but then recoiled in horror when she realised they were fingernails that had been ripped off.

"Ugh, gross." She shuddered.

"This room worse," Gentle Water said, looking at her with slight concern, "but Royston think you need to see."

Amanda took a breath and tried her best to compose herself. "Okay, let's go in," she said. The jumper was doing little to hold off the horrendous stench now. It had seeped through, but she kept it pressed tight against her face anyway.

Stepping down into the room, Gentle Water swept the torch slowly around. Amanda felt increasingly sick as each new horror that this place contained was revealed to her. It was like a slaughterhouse. Dried blood was everywhere, splattered on the walls and floor, while the remains of several dead bodies lay rotting, covered in writhing maggots, and turning black and purple with time.

Limbs had been ripped off, bodies pulverised, chunks bitten out of them, heads crushed, and internal organs, no longer really recognisable, were everywhere.

A vast sarcophagus dominated the centre of the room. It was way too big for a single human, but maybe it could hold Balor or Horlack. What remained of its lid was scattered about the room, and inside, the body of a woman lay rotting, split open from her crotch to her ribcage.

"Feck me," Amanda whispered. "What the hell happened to her?"

"Horlack." Gentle Water said solemnly.

This last sight was too much. Turning away, Amanda vomited her lunch onto the dirt floor. She coughed and spat the half-digested food from her mouth, but now, with the jumper removed from her face, the full strength of the smell assaulted her senses.

"Oh, jaysus," she muttered as she retched again.

She stepped out of the room and sat on the edge of the slab just outside the doorway. She did her best to clean herself up and regain some control over her stomach. Her sweater was ruined, but she didn't care.

"Are we done?" Amanda called out, sitting with her elbows on her knees, leaning forward to spit the last remains of her sick onto the tomb's floor. She barely noticed the smell now.

"Nearly," Gentle Water replied.

With a deep breath, Amanda rose and stepped into the chamber again. Gentle Water stood to one side, his torch angled up at the wall, leaving the rest of the room mercifully shrouded in darkness.

"What's the craic?" Amanda asked, her voice croaky.

"Look," Gentle Water replied.

Getting close, Amanda peered up to see something had been carved into the wall on top of the hieroglyphs in a very rough way. It was a string of words in modern English which read: *Do not lift the slab, Horlack lies within.*

"What the hell?"

"This is mystery, it English, modern English, and yet carving hundreds of years old."

"It's a warning," Amanda said.

"It was," Gentle Water agreed.

Amanda looked into the shadows again, barely making out the shapes of the corpses. "An unheeded warning," she muttered to herself, feeling sorry for the victims of Horlack's rampage. "So, Horlack came from here?"

"Yes. We think he imprisoned here. Before this, before New York when he meet you, he last seen in Fourth Crusade in Constantinople, about eight hundred years ago. He disappear. We think he imprisoned here by someone…"

"Who?"

"We not know."

"So, why me? Why did he attack me in New York?"

"We not know also. Sorry."

Amanda grimaced, she didn't like not knowing these things. But Horlack was gone, so maybe it didn't matter. Whatever that thing had in mind for her, it had failed, and now she was a Magus because of it. Perhaps it was mistaken identity or just a mistake in general. Whatever the reason, it had all worked out in the end.

"So, are we done here?"

"Done," Gentle Water answered, turning and heading back the way they'd come. Before long, they were back out in the desert sun and within moments, out of the Dead Magic Zone.

The rush of power and energy that flooded back into her as she stepped out of the zone was exhilarating and very welcome. She felt connected to the world around her once more.

"I'm glad we're out of there," she said.

"Yes, it good to be out. Let us return to Legacy House, yes?"

Amanda nodded and allowed Gentle Water to Port them both out of the desert and back into the entrance hall of the Legacy House. The Aegis recognised Gentle Water's Magic and allowed him through without a problem.

"Aaah, you're back. Good," Royston said. He'd been waiting for them in the hallway with Raven. "We've picked up some disturbing reports from London about the massacre of three families, including one child. The Albion Coven says there are clear Magical traces there, and our hacker has found that all three sets of parents had kids. Want to take a guess who those kids are?"

"The ones we saw being chased by Angel," Amanda guessed.

"Bingo. The Albion traced them to a London police station, but they're letting us deal with it since we were already involved. I'm sending Raven there to get the kids and bring them here before the Nomads kill them and take whatever it is they have. You went to London with him last time. Do you want to go with him again?"

Amanda smiled. "I do."

"Is that okay with you, Raven?" Royston asked him.

"Of course, shall we go?"

"Absolutely, just give me two seconds to wash my mouth out," Amanda answered. She dashed to the nearest bathroom and sloshed water around her mouth. With a quick working of Magic, she Ported some fresh clothes to the bathroom and changed out of her dirty outfit that smelt of death and vomit.

Feeling better, Amanda returned to the lobby and to Raven who stood waiting for her. "Ready."

"Okay, let's go," Raven answered, Essentia flaring again.

- Internal missive within the Disciples of the Cross.

Grand Inquisitor Damask,

I offer my most sincere apologies. I had the children and the artifact for a short while, but I let them slip my grasp, and they are on the run. All is not lost, however. I have managed to plant a tracking device on the boy, Stephan, and its signal is clean. I am regrouping and readying an attempt to reacquire them as I write this.

The Warlocks are proving to be troublesome, however, and they forced the action I took earlier tonight. I feel I was justified in my efforts and in the loss of life. I have prayed for my fallen comrades, I ask that you might join me.

Please, find attached a full report on the night's events.

May God be with you.

Knight Inquisitor de Luca.

Liberation

London, England

The flash of light in Amanda's vision faded, and she found herself on a rooftop, standing beside Raven. They were on a small flat area next to a skylight, with another man she'd never met waiting close by. Around them, the rest of the rooftop was the typical pitched tiled type that could be seen all around London. The next building over was painted white and stood a few floors taller. Amanda could make out the grey water of the Thames just beyond it, looking cold and uninviting.

Amanda didn't recognise the strange man, but she did recognise the glow coming from him in her Aetheric Sight. He was a Magus and he smiled at them as they appeared. Amanda took half a step back and fed Essentia into her Aegis as she prepared for an attack. Raven hadn't said anything about them meeting anyone.

Raven put his hand on her shoulder. ~It's okay, he's a friend,~ he said to her through the Link.

The man was probably in his fifties with a short salt and pepper beard and a layered tunic that looked like a modern take on a wizard's robes.

He smiled. "Raven," he said in greeting.

"Arch Master Trevelyan," Raven answered. "Are they in there?"

"That's right, and there's some Magic in there too, but I can't get a precise location," he said with a frown. "The Police confiscated an item from them, which we believe to be Magical. It's powerful too and seems to have a disruptive effect on Flux Magic, you won't be able to Port in or out if it's close to you."

"An artifact?" Raven asked, and glanced back at Amanda. "Looks like we were right, they did have something on them back in London."

Amanda nodded, linking this with the artifact that Gentle Water had said was missing from the tomb in Egypt. Somehow, these kids had got hold of it, and now they were way out of their depth.

Gunshots, faint, but certainly there, rang out from the building they were looking at.

"Looks like we don't have time to figure this out," Raven said. "Do you know where they are?"

"The fifth floor," the man said. "Happy hunting." With a sudden whip-crack, he was gone.

Amanda could feel the Essentia flood out of Raven as he worked his Magic. This time, it took a few moments before the rush of energy engulfed them and the typical flash of light in her eyes happened, but soon they were in a stairwell next to a door with 'third floor' imprinted on it.

"Didn't he just say the fifth floor?" Amanda asked.

"Yes, but this is as close as I can get us. Looks like Trevelyan was right about the artifact blocking Flux Magic. "

"Awesome, good to know," she said as Raven started to sprint up the stairs, past people running the other way. The gunfire was much louder in here and echoed through the building. ~What do you think? Nomad?~

~Probably,~ Raven answered through their Link, reaching the fifth floor and charging through the door. People were running everywhere. It was chaos.

~Where do we go?~ Amanda asked as someone pushed past her. People were screaming, the gunfire was very close now.

~No idea, I can't see any concentration of Essentia apart from… Aaah shit, yep, it's another Magus, Nomad probably. He's on the other side of the building.~

Amanda saw it, too. The telltale glow and ripple of Essentia as the Magus used his Magic. But just like Raven, she couldn't pinpoint the artifact that was generating the Flux-blocking effect.

~So, what do we do?~ she asked.

~Read some minds. Someone must know something,~ he answered.

She saw his Magic reach out to people nearby to find the information he needed. Amanda turned and focused elsewhere, doing the same. She reached into a man's head and scanned his memories of the last few hours for anything related to a group of teenagers and some kind of artifact, but found nothing useful. It was done in seconds, so she tried again, reaching into the head of the next person she saw and repeating the process, but still nothing.

The bursts of gunfire continued in the background as Amanda worked her Magic. After her fourth fruitless scan, Raven called out.

"Got them, follow me," he said.

Relief washed over her as she ran after him, pushing through the crowds of people as they charged up a nearby corridor. Raven stopped outside a door, gave it a look as a ripple of Essentia flowed out from him before he lunged forward with a solid kick.

The door flew off its hinges and clattered to the floor just inside. Gunfire sounded again. It was really close, now—maybe one or two rooms away, perhaps three, if they were lucky.

"Raven, we better be quick," she yelped.

Raven ducked into the room, Amanda followed but stopped at the door. She saw three young teenagers, two girls and a boy. They were the same ones that they'd seen the other day in London, but there had been four of them then.

"Who are you?" The boy asked, clearly terrified and clutching his backpack like his life depended on it.

"I'm Raven, this is Amanda, we're here to help you get out of here," he said.

"Hey, you were the ones who helped us with that blonde woman, Angel, right?" the girl with the copper hair asked.

"Bang on," Amanda said, smiling.

"Well, I don't think we need any more help, we just need to get out of here," the boy stated defiantly. "Come on, girls."

"Stephen, I think we should listen to them," the copper-haired girl pleaded with him.

"I'm fed up with listening to people who think they know what's best for us. How do we know these two aren't going to kill us like that man killed Ben? Now, are you coming or what?" Stephen asked, walking past Amanda and giving her an accusing glance.

The two girls followed him, the copper-haired girl leading the way as she continued trying to convince him to think again. "Stephen, they seem to know what they're talking about. Stephen, will you stop and listen to me?"

Amanda turned to Raven. "We need to leave," she said, as another bout of gunfire sounded, shattering glass in the windows above them. A loud bang sounded further up the corridor. Amanda stepped out to take a look and saw a tall, well-muscled and heavily tattooed man step over a police officer he'd just thrown through a door. As he stepped over him, looking up the corridor, he fired his gun into the officer's face, killing him.

One of the girls behind her yelped. Amanda frowned and bolstered her Aegis, staring at this new threat who was glowing with Essentia. If she had to make a guess, she'd bet he was another Nomad.

"Guys, you left the party early," the Nomad accused the teenagers behind her. "And who's the redhead? Have you been making friends?" he asked, his tone light.

Amanda didn't like him, and from the scared noises the three teens were making behind her, it sounded like they didn't like him either.

"I don't know who you are, but they're under our protection now," Amanda replied, doing her best to sound confident and powerful. She wasn't sure it worked, though. She probably just sounded pathetic.

"You don't?" the man asked. "Well, I'm offended. Now, sit down." With a lightning-fast move, he whipped his gun up and fired several times.

Amanda gritted her teeth and clenched her fists as she boosted her Aegis again. The bullets slammed into the large bubble of force that surrounded her and stopped dead, dropping harmlessly to the floor.

Amanda looked up, a huge grin spreading across her face as she realised that her Magic had worked.

"What the hell?" She heard the boy say behind her, along with the squeals and then gasps of the girls.

"So, you've got some skill," the man said, dropping the gun.

Movement to her left caught her eye as Raven, who seemed to have been waiting for the right moment, stepped out into the corridor.

"You're damn right, she has," he replied and worked his Magic. A battering ram of kinetic force slammed into the Nomad and sent him flying back along the corridor. "Check them," Raven said.

Amanda turned and stepped back to the trio. "You guys alright?"

"You... you're... That was... You used..." the boy stammered.

"Magic, yes, we'll explain later, but we have to go. Will you come with us?" Amanda asked. The three of them nodded dumbly. "Raven, we're leaving," she yelled back to him.

"Go," he shouted.

"Come on, quickly." Amanda guided the trio to the stairwell, making sure no one was left behind as they charged down the stairs. Raven followed on behind. Several flights later, Amanda spotted the big green exit sign above the ground floor door. She went for it.

"No, through the wall," Raven shouted at her.

Amanda stopped and looked up. He was pointing to one of the walls. Amanda glanced at it and knew it was an outside wall. With a thought, she raised her hand and threw a powerful, invisible kinetic ram at the wall. Brick and mortar exploded outwards as a huge hole was created right before them.

"Out," Amanda ordered. She looked back to see Raven's mouth hanging agape.

"Howah," he muttered.

"Everything okay?" she asked, not recognising the word. Was it his native tongue?

"Everything's fine. I'm just impressed, that's all," he said.

Amanda couldn't help the smile that played across her lips at his comment. At least, she was impressing him.

"Come on, then, Tonto," Raven said, smiling and running through the hole. They made their way out onto the nearby London street and set off in a southerly direction to the nearest bridge over the Thames. They were soon amongst people and slowed down, their run becoming a brisk walk through the crowds. Amanda couldn't help looking behind her every now and then, checking to see if the Nomad was catching them up.

"What's in that backpack?" Raven asked as they crossed Westminster Bridge.

"Nothing," the boy said, looking back at her and Raven.

"Before we get into that," Amanda said. "I think some introductions are needed. I'm Amanda, this is Raven. What are your names?"

"Why should we tell you?" the boy said.

"I'm Fran, this is my sister Liz, and this grumpy-Guss is Stephen," she said.

Stephen let out an exasperated sigh. "Why did you do that? We don't know who they are."

"I think I can guess they're here to help. After all, they weren't the ones shooting at us," Fran said.

"I don't like it," Stephen answered her.

"You don't have to," Fran said and turned to Raven. "We found an artifact. Stephen bought it in Egypt."

"Fran!" Stephen yelled.

"In Cairo," Liz cut in, clarifying.

"That's right," Fran said. "It's like… it's a golden book filled with writing and we think it might be magical," Fran said.

"Bloody hell." Stephen sighed.

"Magical?" Amanda asked, looking at the backpack. Usually, a Magical item would glow in her Aetheric Sight, but nothing was shining in that bag. There was no concentration of Essentia in there that she could see, and yet she could feel something, something Magical. It was as if the item blocked her Magical sight, but she could still feel the item's presence.

Fran nodded. "Yeah, like, what you were doing back there. We were just trying to figure it out, you know?"

"Fair play to yeh, to be sure," Amanda said. "But, I think you can see that whatever it is, it's in demand, so we need to get it back to our place in Paris. Luckily, that's just a train ride away."

"Can't you just, you know, use some Magic?" Fran asked.

"Usually, but something about this book is preventing that, so if we're going to keep the book, we need to make our way home by other means," Amanda said.

"Train ride it is, then," Fran conceded. Amanda smiled and nodded.

As they walked, Amanda leant in towards Raven and spoke in lower tones. "So, did we lose him? The Nomad, I mean?"

"Nate?"

"That's his name? Nate?"

"Yeah, that's him, and no, I'm doubtful. He wouldn't give up that easily."

"Figured as much," she replied.

Crossing the river, they soon made their way over towards Waterloo Station. It was busy with people waiting for their trains or walking through the platform. Checking the departure boards, there was a Eurostar train leaving shortly for France.

"Okay, let's get over there. Follow me," Raven said. The three teens followed Raven, while Amanda bought up the rear, leaving a gap between herself and Liz, who was the rearmost of the three of them. Raven strode ahead, and as they threaded their way through the crowds, Stephen wasn't able to keep up with him. As another bystander cut through between Stephen and Raven, they all lost sight of him. There were stalls and ticket booths on the concourse, including one just ahead, so he'd probably disappeared around it. Stephen looked back at Amanda, but she nodded for him to keep going.

Amanda hung back a touch more. Something wasn't right here. She wondered if this Nate, the Nomad, would try for the kids here in this very public place.

Stephen led the girls around the next stall. As they turned the corner, someone reached out and grabbed Liz's wrist.

Amanda recognised that muscled, tattooed arm right away. Pulling on Essentia she threw up an illusion. A hologram that hid what was happening and muffled the noise in that area. Liz yelped.

Within a second, Amanda was next to Nate and driving her elbow into the man's face as hard as she could, releasing a burst of Essentia as she did so. Nate's nose exploded in a shower of blood as he fell and dropped back away from her. Suddenly, Raven was there too, catching Nate and guiding him to a chair close by.

"Ace shot there, girl," Raven said. "You were lucky. I think his Aegis was down."

"I thought that was too easy. Why would he do that?"

"So we wouldn't spot him. I walked right past him and had no idea he was there. Stupid *get rezzy apruhan*, thinks he's some kind of big warrior. Hah!"

Amanda turned to the teenagers beside her. "Are you guys okay?"

"Yeah, we're fine. But how come no one saw you do that?" Fran asked, looking around at the oblivious public.

Amanda raised her eyebrows and smiled. "Magic," she said, wiggling her fingers in the air as she said it. "Come on, we can talk more on the train."

Twenty minutes later, the high-speed Eurostar was zipping along the track and leaving London behind with Raven, the three kids, and herself aboard. They found a more or less empty carriage and sat themselves down. Amanda sat beside Raven, while the three teenagers sat opposite them at a table—Liz was beside the window, while Stephen took the aisle seat, with Fran in-between.

~Do you think we'll make it all the way back?~ Amanda asked Raven through their Link.

~Maybe. Nate will have to do some hunting to find us now, but it's not impossible. We're not home free yet, I don't think,~ Raven answered.

~I was thinking the same thing,~ Amanda agreed. Until they were inside the Legacy House, Amanda wouldn't feel totally safe.

She'd seen enough to know that the Nomads and the Inquisitors would not give up that easily.

She looked over at the three teenagers they'd brought with them. She guessed they were maybe around fifteen or sixteen, not much younger than she was really, but despite this, they still looked young to her. Young and vulnerable. They also seemed quite nervous, which given their situation, was entirely understandable.

Now that they were well underway, Amanda leant forward, placing her elbows on the table, and looked Stephen in the eyes. "Hey, how's she cuttin'?"

"Sorry, what?" Stephen asked.

"Oh, sorry," She said, realising they probably didn't understand her Irish slang. "I mean, how are you doing?"

"We're good," Stephen admitted, clearly still a little reluctant to talk to her.

"Ignore him," Fran cut in with a smile. "We're okay. Tired, scared, but alright." Fran was holding Liz in her arms, and Amanda noticed the silent tears gliding down her face.

"I'm sorry you have to go through this," Amanda offered. "I know it's tough. I lost some friends recently, too. But it will get easier, trust me."

They sat there in silence for a while, each of them deep in thought. Amanda kept thinking back to her friends. Howie was still alive and living in New York. She wanted to go and see him sometime. Those early days living at his place had been some of the best she'd had in Manhattan. He'd been fixing up his motorbike in the block's garage. She'd lost count of the times she'd sat there chatting with him and passing him tools as he worked. He'd even taken her out on a bike as well. She'd loved it and had been starting to develop an interest and love for motorcycles herself.

She'd see him again. She was sure of that. As much as she liked Paris and felt at home and relaxed in Ireland, she still knew that her heart would pull her back to the Big Apple. She loved it there. She wondered if she could return someday soon and make a home there.

"So, you can use Magic, right?" Fran asked quietly.

"We can, to be sure. But, um, you don't seem that surprised that Magic is real."

"We've had some experiences, so we knew it was a thing," Fran explained. "But your ability with it is, frankly, amazing."

"Well, we call ourselves Magi, and it's what we do."

"Magi? Are there a lot of you around?"

"My mentor said there were around fifteen thousand on the planet, split into three main groups. The Arcadians, that's us," Amanda explained, pointing to herself and Raven, "the Nomads, who are fairly horrible people, and the Inquisition, who aren't too friendly to us, either."

"So, you're the good guys?" Stephen asked.

"That's my view on it. We're not perfect, but yeah. Let's just say that we have the best of intentions towards the Riven."

"The what?" Stephen asked.

"Normal humans. The none-Magi people," she clarified with a smile.

"Shit, I had no idea," Fran exclaimed. Liz had sat up a little and was taking an interest now. Amanda also noticed that Stephen seemed to be listening intently as well.

"Look," Stephen began. "I'm sorry. I know I've been a bit, well, you know…"

"I know," Amanda replied.

"I'm just… I don't know. It's just a really freaky situation."

"I get it, I understand. We'd like to help you, but we can only do that if you help us."

"Okay, sure," he sighed, his demeanour less confrontational. "What can I do?"

"Can you show me the artifact?" Amanda suggested.

He nodded and pulled his backpack onto his lap. He checked around to make sure no one was looking, and opened the bag with the zip, revealing the metallic golden book inside.

Raven sat up to get a look at it, too.

"Wow." Amanda gasped. "That's really a golden book. And you found it in Egypt?"

"At a market stall. The trader seemed keen to get rid of it, so I bought it from him. But it didn't look like this then. It was encased in a sandstone slab that was covered in carvings. There are photos on my phone, I'll show you later," he continued. "Anyway, it got dropped, and this is what was inside the stone."

"Well, whatever it is, some powerful people are very interested in it. So, we need to get you somewhere safe.

Somewhere where they can't reach you quite as readily, and I'm afraid you won't be able to keep the artifact. Not if you want to live beyond today," Amanda explained.

Stephen looked offended and quite possessive over it.

"It's okay, you keep it for now; we can talk about that later," she said, with a gentle smile, knowing that he wasn't going to give it up easily.

The train soon shot into the tunnel beneath the English Channel. As they talked, Amanda looked at the photos of the sandstone slab on Stephen's phone before handing the device back. The rest of the trip was uneventful and they arrived in Paris without issue. On the train, they'd arranged for a car to be waiting for them at the station. Raven got into the driver's seat and soon they were on their way across Paris towards the Legacy Coven House.

Sitting in the front passenger seat, Amanda kept a lookout around them, scanning for any hint of danger or of any Magi close by, but saw nothing.

When a large flatbed truck shot out in front of them, they were too close to it to stop and rammed into the side of it with an almighty crunch. Another car slammed into their rear end with a second bang, shoving them up against the truck again. Amanda pumped more Essentia into her Aegis as the man in the truck leant out of the window holding an assault rifle and opened fire on their windscreen.

The front of the car erupted in explosions of glass, metal, and fabric as bullets rained down on herself and Raven.

Amanda yelped, panicking for a moment, terrified that the gunfire would rip her to shreds, but her Aegis held firm, stopping the metal slugs, dead.

Magic flared close by as more men surrounded the car. The rear passenger door flung itself open. Stephen, still gripping his backpack, yelled as he was ripped from the back seat by an invisible force.

The girls screamed. Too late, Amanda and Raven pushed their Aegises out to include the girls, two seconds before the men who had surrounded the vehicle opened fire.

The girls screamed again. Bullets slammed into the Aegis. Although it held, for now, Amanda knew right away that these shells were infused with Essentia and were damaging their shields.

"We gotta go," Raven shouted, "this is too much."

"Agreed. Go, let's get out of here," Amanda called out over the cacophony of gunfire and bullet hits. She looked back to see a man pulling Stephen away from the car. The thug grabbed the bag and handed it over to another man, who glowed with Essentia, marking him as a Magus. He was a Magus she recognised as well. It was the man from the airport who'd attempted to kidnap her. "Shit, I recognise him. It's the Inquisition."

The girls were screaming for Stephen in the back of the car. Fran went to climb out, but Liz held her back. Amanda grabbed her, too. Losing one was bad enough, she didn't want to lose another.

"No, stay here," Amanda called out, but she wasn't sure Fran was listening. Raven's Magic flared beside her as the car continued to be peppered with bullets. Looking forward, Amanda saw that the truck which had been blocking their exit was gone, having been lifted away by Raven's Magic. Raven floored it and sped away, wheels spinning with a high-pitched squeal as he went. Looking back, Amanda watched the truck fall back to earth just behind them and land on the other car that had been blocking them in from behind.

As they sped through the streets, the girls were sobbing in the back, upset that Stephen was gone. Amanda leant towards them as the car bumped along the road.

"We'll get him back. We'll find him, I promise," she reassured them.

"You promise?" Fran asked, sniffing back tears.

"You have my word."

- An internal missive within the Disciples of the Cross.

Inquisitor de Luca,

Congratulations on retrieving the artifact from the apprentice Witches. Please be advised, I am in Paris and will meet you at the Gare de Bercy train station where we have an Inquisitorial car to ourselves. Please make all haste.

Mary Damask

***

- An internal message within the Black Knights Coven.

Baal Yasmin, it's come to my attention that High Inquisitor Damask has commandeered a train carriage in Paris to guard the transportation of some kind of artifact. I thought this might be of interest to you.

Your loyal servant, Raphaella Tanzi

***

- London, England

Angel opened the mental Link that she could sense in her mind.

~Xander,~ she sent through it. ~What can I do for you?~

~Nothing really. Not right now, anyway. It's more about what I can do for you,~ Xander replied.

~Really. Do you have some information for me by any chance?~

~Yasmin, it appears, has boarded a train heading south from Paris with her Apprentice, Nate. As best as I can find out, there's something on the train that they want.~

Angel smiled as Xander's report matched some intel that her coven had obtained from their contacts in the Vatican.

~Do you know what it might be?~ Xander asked.

~Yes,~ she said and closed the Link. "I do," she finished out loud, pulling on the Magical energies around her.

Boarding Action

Paris, France

Amanda led the girls down into the basement level of the Legacy House and into a large room. There were several people already there including Raven, Gentle Water, Royston, and two others she wasn't familiar with.

The girls looked a little nervous, but at least they'd calmed down. Amanda had taken the girls off to get them cleaned up and left Raven to explain the events of the last few hours to Royston.

It had taken Amanda a while to get the girls to relax a little and to reassure them they were doing everything that they could. The Inquisition would be taking the gold book to the Vatican and would be unable to Port it there, which meant they had time. Once the girls understood this, it seemed to help their mood and they showered while Amanda conjured up some new clothes for them.

It wasn't long after that when Royston called her down to the operations room in the basement of the house. Like all the rooms in the Legacy Mansion, it was a large affair with banks of computers and oversized screens on one wall with a table at the back.

It looked like something out of a science-fiction movie with floating holograms of light hanging above the table showing maps and other data. The girls were awestruck.

"Ah, welcome," Royston greeted her. "I trust we're all cleaned up now?"

Amanda nodded. "We are. So, has there been any progress?"

"Actually, yes," Royston revealed. "Ekkehardt Möller is our resident hacker. He's been in touch with his contacts on the Dark Web as well as monitoring the transport hubs, and we think we've found them."

Amanda glanced over at the man sitting in front of a huge bank of computer monitors. She hadn't met Möller before or heard of the Dark Web, whatever that might be, but she understood what hacking was and that was good enough for her.

"So, where is he?" Fran blurted out the second Royston had finished his sentence.

Royston smiled, ignoring the lack of manners. "We think he's on a train. That train, to be precise," he said, pointing to a screen on the wall. It showed a top-down view of a train speeding through the countryside.

"A train? Okay, not what I expected," Amanda commented.

"The Inquisitors have the rear-most car all to themselves," Royston continued. "It's protected by an Aegis, of course, but the golden book you described is frustrating our attempts at scrying anyway. The closest we can scry, and the nearest anyone Porting in can get, would be two or three carriages away up the train from the Inquisitor's car."

"It's heading south?" Amanda asked.

"All the way to Rome, yes."

Amanda nodded. "So, what is this golden book? What does it do that makes it so valuable?"

"Maybe I can answer that." The other man in the room she hadn't met before stepped forward. He looked to be in his fifties, maybe, with greying hair, dusky skin, and a heavily lined face, but Amanda could feel the raw Magical power flowing out from him. He wasn't hiding his Magical strength at all.

"This is Israel Roth, one of the Arch Masters affiliated with this coven," Royston introduced him.

"Greetings," Israel said to Amanda. He had a slight Middle Eastern accent, which gave him a cultured air. "It's a pleasure to meet you. Roy here speaks highly of you. It seems you have impressed everyone with your ability, young lady. I'm looking forward to watching you grow into your power."

Amanda smiled with gratitude and humility. "Ah, well, thank you, it's not a bother. I hope I don't disappoint you, to be sure."

"I seriously doubt that," he answered with a friendly smile. "The book you seek is an ancient Magical artifact, that is well known amongst Magi scholars, but it has not been seen in centuries. It's last known location was in Constantinople, in 1204. It went missing during the fourth crusades sack of that city. Incidentally, that was also the last time and place anyone saw Horlack before he attacked you in New York."

"Interesting," Amanda answered. It seemed like the two things were linked somehow, given that the book was found in the tomb Horlack had been released from. She didn't know how they were connected through and returned to her earlier question. "And the book? What can it do?"

"The book grants the reader the ability to turn any Riven human into a Magus."

"It turns people into Magi?" Amanda asked, stunned.

Israel nodded. "Which is why we cannot allow it to fall into the hands of the Nomads, or the Inquisition."

"They would swell their ranks within days, and turn the tide of the war," Royston explained.

Amanda now understood the stakes and knew they had to get that book back. "I agree, we have to get it back."

"And Stephen," Fran added.

Amanda smiled at the young woman. "Of course."

"So, what's the plan?" Fran asked.

"We go and get him, of course," Raven answered, stepping into the discussion. "Myself, Gentle Water, and, if you're feeling up to it, you," he directed this last word to Amanda, "will Port over there and take on the Inquisitors."

Amanda allowed herself a slight smile. She felt quite flattered that they'd included her in another mission. "After what they did to us in the car? I'm in."

"Excellent," Raven exclaimed. "My thoughts exactly."

"Are you sure us three can do this?" Amanda asked. "What about Xain, Orion, and the others?"

"They're on another mission currently, but the Inquisitors have a limited grasp of Magic. Given how they view it as a gift from God, they tend to use it sparingly and fight with more conventional weapons. You should be able to take them on," Royston reassured her.

"Any Nomads on the train?" Amanda asked.

"Not that we can see," Royston replied.

"That's not a no," Amanda commented.

"No, it isn't, so watch your back."

"Are you ready?" Raven asked.

"We're coming, too," Fran cut in, stepping forward with Liz on her heels.

"Excuse me?" Raven asked in surprise.

"He's our friend, we need to be there," Fran continued.

Amanda turned towards them. "Look," she began, taking hold of Fran's hands, "that's not a great idea. This will be a dangerous fight…"

"And not our first. We're going with you," Fran cut in, fierce determination in her eyes and face.

Amanda straightened up and looked at the girls. Fran was the more confident of the pair, but she could see they were both set on this idea. She had to admit, if she were in their position, she'd want to go along as well. How could she stop them from doing whatever they possibly could to save their friend, when being passive and not using her magic to save her friend, not doing whatever she possibly could, had lost her Georgina? Besides, they were old enough to choose for themselves.

"Okay, sure, you can come," she relented.

"What?" Raven yelled. "Are you crazy?"

Amanda turned to him. "Possibly, but I can see it from their point of view. They're sixteen, Raven, they can make this decision for themselves. If they want to come, that's their choice, not ours. They know how dangerous it will be."

"And you're only nineteen, I'm not sure you should be…"

"Amanda is right," Gentle Water cut in.

"I agree," Royston added.

Raven backed off and raised his hands. "Okay, sure, but we're not babysitting them. They'll have to take care of themselves."

"Agreed." Amanda turned to the twins. "This is your choice, you're old enough to make your own decisions, okay? It will be dangerous, so keep your distance and let us do what we do best, got it?"

Both girls nodded, Fran with more enthusiasm than Liz.

"Okay, so, you ready?" Amanda asked.

The twins looked at each other and then back at Amanda.

"Yes," they said at once.

"Then let's go and kick some arse," Amanda enthused. "So, um, how are we doing this?"

Israel will Port you all over there, as close to the Inquisitor's car as he can."

"Indeed," Israel added. "So, let's not delay this mission any further. Are you ready?"

Everyone nodded or agreed, and within moments, there was a snap of air and she found herself stood on the train. They were in one of the vestibule areas at the end of a carriage where it attached to the next wagon with a flexible joint. There were exit doors on either side of the compartment leading off the train, and sliding doors at either end of the chamber that led into each train car. No one else was in here, even the toilet stalls were empty.

"Wow, that was insane," Fran exclaimed. Amanda looked over at the girls and the expression of wonder and excitement that had appeared on their previously sullen faces. It was the first time they'd experienced Porting, and it seemed to have distracted them. Leaving them to their moment of excitement, Amanda turned to Raven and Gentle Water.

"Looks like we made it," Amanda observed.

"Yep, and our target is two carriage lengths that way," Raven replied, looking towards the back of the train.

"Do you think they noticed us arrive?" she asked as she looked through the windows set in each door, up the centre of the carriages towards the Inquisitorial car.

"Only one way to find out," Raven answered opening the door to the carriage. Amanda followed Gentle Water, who was following Raven, and made sure the girls stayed close to her. The train wasn't busy, but it wasn't empty, either. She walked past people of all ages, sitting in their seats and enjoying the ride. She didn't like the idea of them getting hurt and hoped what they were about to do wouldn't put any of them into the hospital. Or worse.

The walk up the length of the two train cars was uneventful, and there were no apparent Magical effects between where they appeared and the end carriage, which glowed with an Aegis of Essentia all around it.

Amanda sent a pulse of energy through the Link to Gentle Water and Raven, signalling to them that she wanted to talk. The communal Link opened up.

~So, how do we do this?~ she asked as they walked. ~We have an Aegis to break through up here.~

~I say we synchronise our attack on their Aegis and go in hard and fast. We need to break that Aegis as quickly as we can,~ Raven stated.

~That sounds like good plan to me,~ Gentle Water answered, his voice loud and clear in her mind.

~Agreed.~ Amanda started to pull in Essentia, drawing it into her body, ready to use in their attack. Her Aegis was already at full strength and she was as prepared as she would ever be for the fight that was about to happen.

Finally, they walked through the sliding door that led to the adjoining compartment between this and the Inquisitor's car. The compartment was empty and the door at the far side of the vestibule was blacked out. A sign on it proclaimed it to be strictly for authorised persons only. The Aegis barrier was just outside that door and glowed gold in Amanda's vision.

She felt the twins press into the compartment behind her and turned to face them, remembering they were there. She looked back into the previous carriage and saw empty seats. "Girls, I need you to go and sit in there. This is about to get dangerous and I don't want you getting hurt, okay?"

"But, we can help," Fran protested.

"I know you think you can, but honestly, just let us do our job," Amanda pleaded.

Fran sighed, but agreed, leading Liz back out of the compartment and into the first free seats they could find.

Satisfied they were safe, Amanda turned back and stepped up next to her two friends.

"Ready?" Raven asked.

"As I'll ever be," Amanda answered. Gentle Water nodded.

Raven counted down. "Okay, then, three, two, one, now," A massive rush of energy flooded out of all three of them. Essentia blasted the Inquisitors' Aegis, hammering against its shell, trying to overload it and break it down.

It took a few heart-pounding seconds, but it faltered and then shattered entirely, disappearing from their Aetheric Sight.

Raven didn't seem to take a breath before striding forward and giving the door a solid kick. Like most Magi, Raven's strength was enhanced, and the door flew off its hinges into the well-lit interior of the Inquisitors' car, banging to the floor before a small crowd of men and women in black fatigues, padding, armour, and webbing, holding various weapons, but mainly swords. They looked like a SWAT team with a fetish for medieval weaponry.

Raven charged in without waiting, followed by Gentle Water. Amanda hesitated for half a second, a flicker of doubt passing through her mind when she saw the mob of people in there wanting to cut her to ribbons, but it was gone as quick as it appeared, and she ran into the carriage.

One of the Crusaders dodged around Raven, stepped up onto a side bench and leapt at Amanda, swinging his Essentia-laced blade at her. It sang as it whipped through the air, missing her as she dodged away.

Their weapons, including their guns, if her Magical sight was to be believed, were infused with Magical energy, meaning their strikes would damage her Aegis and hurt like a mother-fecker if they actually hit her.

The Crusader swung his blade back and forth, again and again, forcing Amanda back until she spotted a gap in his defence and stepped in with a solid jab to his face.

She felt his nose crack as she landed the punch. He staggered back.

Three more Crusaders had followed the first to her, and one of them leapt forward over his falling teammate and shoulder barged her, ramming into her flank.

Amanda cursed under her breath as she fell. That was an idiot move, she thought, leaving herself open like that. She moved with the fall, though, and rolled backwards, through the door, and back out into the vestibule. In a single beat of her heart, she was up again as the Crusader lunged, stabbing at her with his blade as he stepped through the small doorway. Amanda dodged, kicked out, and heard his knee crunch.

The man yelled in pain. The other two that were after her followed their comrade, looking for a way to reach her. Amanda heard the door behind her open and looked to see Fran and Liz in the doorway.

Shit, she thought, what are they doing here? She needed to get these Crusaders away from the twins. With a swipe of her hands and a working of Magic, the Crusader with the fractured knee flew sideways and smashed through the side exit door to Amanda's left with a loud bang of wrenching metal and shattering glass.

She looked up at the two remaining Crusaders. They were utterly focused on her and looked furious beyond words on seeing their companion get thrown from the train.

"Come on," Amanda yelled at them and ran towards the exit door she'd created as the two Crusaders stepped out. Amanda leapt, caught hold of the top of the door, and swung herself up and around, landing on top of the moving train.

The wind whipped past her, sending her hair flying and her skirt flapping, ruining any modesty she still had. Backing off towards the front of the train, Amanda hoped her gamble would pay off, and the two Crusaders would follow her up, ignoring the twins.

As she waited, she concentrated and used an effect that her mentor had told her was called Multi-tasking. The Magic split her mind into several parts—in her case three—each entirely independent and able to use Magic individually, while still working as a whole rather than at cross-purposes. She'd yet to use it in a real fight, but now seemed like a good time.

Another second later, and the first of the two Crusaders jumped up onto the roof, landing in a crouch. A beat later, and the second one appeared—a female who looked just as angry as the first.

The man ran at her, holding his sword ready, but he was furious and off-balance. Calmly, Amanda spun around him, dodging him entirely, flicking one of her feet out to pull one of his out from under him. Giving him an elbow jab into his kidneys at the same time, she released a shock of Essentia as she did it.

The Crusader stumbled and fell behind her as the woman swung at her.

Dodging again, Amanda slapped the weapon away and drove the heel of her hand into the girl's jaw. Hearing an audible crack, Amanda followed with an elbow into her sternum, knocking the wind out of her. With her opponent off balance, Amanda swiped her leg. Her booted foot caught the Crusader's leg, and suddenly nothing was holding her upright. The Crusader hit the roof of the carriage face first with a grunt.

She heard footsteps behind her.

Amanda spun to see the first Crusader run and then leap at her, sword held ready. Essentia whipped out as she bent it to her will and kinetic energy hit the Knight side-on, sending him flying into a passing tree trunk with a rather sickening thud.

"No!" yelled the Crusader behind her. The woman jumped to her feet, brandished her sword and charged, screaming. "I'll cut you in half for that."

Amanda turned, called on her Essentia again and sent a bolt of blue lightning at her. The powerful blast struck the Knight in the chest, knocking her down with a savage yell and a grunt before hitting the roof of the carriage. She didn't get up again.

Amanda just stood there for a moment, looking down at the body of the Crusader Knight with the huge burn mark on her chest.

"Feck me," Amanda muttered. "Was it worth it?" Predictably, there was no answer. Amanda just shook her head and took a breath, knowing she'd better get back in there and help her friends.

Amanda found the door and swung back inside, landing in the vestibule in a crouch. She looked back into the passenger car, but couldn't see Fran or Liz.

Frowning and wondering where they might be, she stepped into the Inquisitors' car. Fran and Liz were in there, standing between her and the fight that Raven and Gentle Water were engaged in with their backs to her. Bodies of unconscious or maybe dead Crusaders, beaten into submission by Raven and Gentle Water, lay scattered over the floor, but they still had a small army to deal with.

What were the girls doing? she wondered. The fight ebbed and flowed, and when a gap opened up around the side, the girls, led by Fran, darted around the action.

She guessed the Knights didn't see them as a threat and ignored them.

Moving inside, Amanda peered through the fight to try and see what the girls were doing.

Suddenly, she spotted Vito standing alongside a stiff-looking woman with a bob of black hair in some fairly fancy ecclesiastical robes. Nearby, the golden book lay on the table closest to Vito and the woman. Sitting near them on the opposite side was Stephen.

She couldn't hear anything with all the shouting and fighting, but she saw the girls step forward and shout at the Inquisitors. Vito immediately pulled his sword and strode towards the girls, its blade glowing brightly with Magical energy in her Aetheric Sight.

Before Amanda could react, Essentia flared from the girls in a powerful wave of energy that rushed out of the pair. They were holding hands, fierce determination making their spines straight and their heads held high.

The side of the train exploded out, taking Vito with it. The shockwave slammed the woman against the far wall, where she slumped, unconscious.

The train braked hard and lurched to a sudden and jarring stop that sent everyone staggering until it finally came to rest. The screeching, juddering stop sent most of the people in the train sprawling to the floor, Amanda included, as she tried to keep an eye on the girls.

Amanda saw Fran and Liz get back up off the floor after having fallen and run for Stephen. Amanda lost sight of them as another Crusader broke free from the fight and ran at her, his sword swinging. Jumping to her feet, Amanda ducked under the blade and slammed her elbow into his stomach before standing up and shoulder barging him away.

The man staggered back and stood up to find a gun pressed against his temple. Amanda looked on in shock. Angel, having just entered the carriage, was taking aim at the Knight.

The gun fired with a flash of golden energy from the Essentia-powered bullet. The crusader died instantly, with half his head missing.

Angel didn't hesitate and turned the gun on Amanda.

Amanda lashed out, knocking the gun sideways and out of Angel's grip. The look on Angel's face was wonderful, she thought. Confusion and shock played over the Nomad's features for a second, but Amanda wasn't going to stand there and enjoy it. She turned and kicked out, bringing her foot up high across Angel's face. She spun a second time, getting a follow-up kick in and then another in a jumping boost as she flipped again before landing, turning, and swinging her foot in for a fourth strike.

Angel caught it in a vice-like grip.

"My turn," she said and twisted Amanda's leg. She was too strong to resist and would have broken or dislocated something, so Amanda went with it and flipped herself over, kicking out with her other booted foot.

Her quick thinking must have caught Angel by surprise because she released Amanda's foot and cursed.

Essentia flared and Amanda was thrown back against the rear wall, her Aegis crackling as it fought off the attack.

Amanda pushed herself up off the floor where she'd landed. She finally got her feet under her, only to be knocked back and then lifted up from the floor by more Magic. Meanwhile, three or four more flares of Essentia were blasting out of Angel and hitting Amanda's Aegis, breaking it down, and keeping her pinned to the wall.

Angel looked up at her and cocked her head sideways. "My dear, you're not quite at a level that you can stand up to me. This little fight has been fun, but I think this lesson is over," she said with a smile that Amanda did not like.

Amanda fed even more Essentia into her Aegis, but she couldn't build it up as fast as Angel could rip it down.

Pinned against the wall, a foot above the floor, Angel's Magic hammered against her Shield. It was an unstoppable force slamming into her and trying to crush and obliterate her.

Amanda did her best to push back with her own Magic, but Angel was way more skilled than she was. What she lacked in skill though, she made up for in raw power. She might not be equal in rank to Angel, but her connection to Essentia was a strong one.

Opening her eyes, Amanda saw that Angel wasn't even looking at her anymore. She was looking out over the room, past the fight Raven and Gentle Water were still engaged in. More Essentia flared and the golden book that Liz had since grabbed, started to float, dragging Liz with it as it rose up to move over the top of the fight.

Liz yelped.

Gentle Water looked back at Amanda, doing his best to fend off two Crusaders while he was distracted by Amanda's plight.

Raven spotted Liz, and Amanda saw Magic flare out of him towards Liz as they did their best to resist Angel's pull.

Amanda struggled to breathe. The attack was breaking through her Aegis and crushing her lungs. The pressure forced air out of her chest and squeezed her throat.

As she struggled to catch a breath, her vision began to tunnel. Black nothingness crept into the edges of her sight as she gasped for air, but found none.

Images flashed through her mind. Memories of her time in the orphanage, of her friend Alicia who had been there for her when no one else had. Howie in New York who had taken her in, cared for her, and given her some hope. Georgina who had helped her when she needed it and had become one of her best friends in the process, even if their life on the streets wasn't exactly ideal.

And, of course, Gentle Water, who was looking at her now with desperate concern. The Knights who fought him took advantage of his distraction and pressed the fight as she thought back over the last two years of her training.

Her mentor had brought her through the grief of losing her friends and shown her the world was bigger and stranger than she could ever have imagined.

She didn't want to lose that and made a promise to herself that if she ever got out of this, she would live her life the best way she knew how. She would throw herself into this world of

Magic and become the best she could be. It was what Georgina would have wanted.

The blackness closed in as the scene before her shrunk away, fading into nothingness.

Light, blinding and powerful, flared up from the darkness as she dropped to the floor. Amanda pulled in a great lungful of air in a laboured gasp. She took another breath and then suddenly remembered the danger she was surrounded by and looked up.

Angel was on her knees, looking as if she'd been slammed with a momentous attack that had wiped her out. She lifted her head and cowered as a figure in black stepped into the carriage.

Amanda recognised her right away. It was the woman from the museum, Yasmin, and she did not look happy as she stared down at Angel.

She wasn't in the slinky dress anymore, though. Instead, she wore a strange fitted, black catsuit, or at least, that's what it looked like. It had a peculiar pearlescent quality to it and ended at her wrists and neck as it if were liquid, with glistening black runnels of it reaching down to her hands and up to her jaw.

She still had that lustrous, wavy, jet-black hair with purple streaks that framed her angular face.

She stopped just inside the doorway, with Nate appearing in the opening just behind her.

"Yasmin…" Angel gasped under her breath.

"Angel," Yasmin replied, her tone cold and sharp. "Always getting in my way."

"My Baal, my utmost apologies, I didn't…"

"Shut up," Yasmin barked, having turned her head sideways to look at Amanda.

Getting to her feet, Amanda looked back, using her hand to steady herself against the wall as she regained her balance on wobbly legs.

"Curious," Yasmin said to herself quietly.

"What are you doing here?" Amanda asked.

Yasmin let out a breath and raised her eyebrows with a look that said, really?

Amanda glanced left at the golden book still in Liz's arms, as her mentor and Raven finished off the last of the Knights nearby.

With unsteady feet, Amanda stepped over the bodies of Crusaders and stepped up next to Liz. Yasmin watched her move, tracking her like a hungry cat watches a bird.

Amanda put her arm around Liz as she pumped Essentia into her Aegis, mending its broken shell and giving her and Liz a modicum of protection. She knew it was relatively pointless, though. If Angel could best her, then Yasmin, an Arch Magus by all accounts, would destroy her.

"You'll need to go through me if you want this book," Amanda challenged her, terrified, but resolute.

"Whoever said I wanted the book or wanted to hurt you?" Yasmin asked. Essentia surged and Angel—protesting and struggling all the while—rose up from the floor in a curled up ball to hover beside Yasmin.

"I'll see you soon, Miss Page," Yasmin said, and the roof of the train above her exploded out, allowing Yasmin, Nate, and Angel to rise up through it in a flash, leaving Amanda and her friends alone.

"What was all that about?" Liz asked.

"Honestly, I'm not sure. I thought she wanted the book, so I did," Amanda mused. Something wasn't right here. She couldn't put her finger on it, though. Why would Yasmin come here, and then just leave? She couldn't believe it was to kidnap Angel—that was surely just a coincidence… "Well, it's not a problem to think about right now. How're Fran and Stephen?" she asked, turning to see where they were.

She saw them right away, embracing each other and sharing a kiss. Amanda relaxed, pleased they were unharmed.

Movement behind them, hidden by their bodies, confused Amanda for a moment until she spotted the woman who had been with Vito and who'd been knocked unconscious by the Magic the twins had used, running at the young couple.

The woman swung her sword, bringing it down into the back of Stephen's neck and through Fran's in a single, Magic-infused slash.

The woman changed direction and bolted sideways as the two teenagers stood there for a second, slowly falling away from each other as their heads tipped over and fell from their shoulders to hit the floor before their bodies did the same. The thuds on the floor of the train car as the two heads bounced and rolled to a stop, trailing blood was sickening.

The woman leapt from the train in a swan dive and disappeared out of the hole. Amanda ran over and stopped at the edge of the ragged hole in the side of the carriage. The train had stopped on top of an aqueduct and was easily over a hundred feet above the valley floor below. The woman had gone, disappeared, but Amanda suspected that would not be the last they'd hear from her.

Behind her, Liz wailed. Everything she knew had been violently ripped from her. Amanda went to her. She held the broken teenager in her arms and said nothing. She would simply be there for her from this day forward.

- Nephilim Industries report by Michael on the missing CEO Angel Alergeri.

It's been two weeks now with no contact from her, which for Angel, is unusual. We are actively hunting for her now and following up on the last leads we had of her.

Our informant within Yasmin's organisation has also disappeared and may have been discovered. Which, likely means he's dead.

Further reports will be made as things develop.

Moving on

Donegal, Ireland

Amanda leant against the fence that surrounded her cottage, resting her arms on the top beam, and looking out over the hills that surrounded her little home. It was a warm day and Amanda had broken out one of her sundresses. It was a plain white one, with thin shoulder straps, and a thigh-length skirt that the wind caught and played with.

It had been a few weeks since the events on the train, and they had decided that some time here at the cottage was just what Liz needed. It was calm here, away from the stresses of day-to-day life and well away from anything that might bring back painful memories.

Amanda thought that she had at least some idea about how Liz felt. She hadn't lost a twin sister, of course, but she felt sure she could help a little bit and provide some perspective.

She remembered the day that Georgina had told her she was HIV positive and that she had only months, maybe weeks, to live. She remembered the tears, the anger, and the frustration at the unfairness of it.

Seeing her friend go through that, seeing her deteriorate and become a shell of her former self had been like living through a nightmare. It was so unfair, and yet, with the work they did on the streets of New York, they knew the risks. Georgina had been careless and had missed a few of her medicals, which might have picked it up sooner. What Amanda did know with absolute certainty, was that Georgina would want her to keep on living her life. She would want her to be the best she could be, to throw herself into this fantastic adventure, and to help others whenever she could.

She'd made a promise to Georgina the day they'd buried her that she would keep going, that she would live the best life she could, for both of them, and she hoped that by doing so, she would make her friend proud of her.

Her subsequent discovery of Magic had initially made her question her choices, and despair at the thought that she could have saved her friend.

Gentle Water had helped with that, and after the events on the train, Amanda knew that her promise to Georgina was even more relevant now, than it had ever been. She didn't want to just sit by and do nothing anymore.

After seeing her use Magic on the train, Amanda and some of the Legacy Magi had taken a closer look at Liz. It turned out she was a latent, untrained Magus. Her sister had probably been one as well. Amanda had decided right away that she would train her. She would be Liz's mentor and hoped that the process of learning Magic would aid in the grieving and healing process, too.

It was still very early days, but she was already confident she was seeing some progress.

She had since learned that the woman who had killed Fran and Stephen was Mary Damask, one of the Inquisition's

Conclave of High Inquisitors, the leaders of the Inquisition. She was a dedicated and ruthless individual. Amanda did not like the sound of her at all.

As she enjoyed the sunshine, she looked back towards the house to see Liz wandering around the garden, lost in thought, kicking a stone, and enjoying some time to herself. Amanda had been careful not to crowd her, but to be there for her when she needed company.

Essentia flared close by, as Amanda had expected, and Gentle Water appeared out of thin air just outside the fence, which also marked the outer edge of the cottage's Aegis that Amanda had been working on.

"Morning," Amanda greeted her friend.

"Hello, Amanda," he said, before noticing Liz off in the distance. Liz looked up once and waved before returning to her thoughts. "How is she?"

"She's fine. It's still very raw for her, so it will take a while, but I'm confident she'll get there. I've not seen you much these past few weeks. Is everything okay?"

"Everything is… Grand, as you say."

Amanda smiled. "Happy days. Are you coming back to stay with us for a bit?"

"Yes, if you happy to have me," he said.

"Liz needs to get used to other people being around, so I think it's a good idea." Amanda nodded before she turned back to him. "So, that was a bleedin' full-on introduction to the world of the Magi."

"Sorry?"

"The train. Shite got crazy there for a moment," she clarified.

Gentle Water nodded. "It was crazy time, yes. Sorry."

"No, don't apologise. I don't regret being a part of it. Our intentions were honourable and we did our best. If Fran and Liz had stayed back and listened to us, maybe things would have been different, to be sure, but what's done is done."

"Indeed, very wise," Gentle Water agreed.

Amanda nodded. She remembered his teachings on Time Magic and the mysterious Weavers—beings who patrolled the timeline and stopped careless Magi from damaging it. She did not fancy disappearing without a trace for doing something silly.

"Exactly, all we can do is move forward and make the best of it. So, what's next on the agenda for a young Magus such as me, GW?" she asked with a smile.

Her mentor joined in her smile. "More than you could ever imagine."

Epilogue

Crystal walked gingerly through the doors of the prison fortress, pushing them open a little wider with both hands. Beyond those enormous black doors, veiled in shadow, waited the vaulted entrance hall. The darkness within was compounded by the walls of black, glass-like brick that glistened in the weak light. Around the walls, corridors snaked off into the murky depths. But Crystal's attention was focused on a mound on the floor up ahead.

Using her Aetheric Sight to pierce the darkness, she felt sure she was alone in here, with only the corpse of her friend in the room with her.

Sweeping her gaze left and right, she approached the remains nervously. She'd been inside the fortress many times to monitor the inmates the prison held. But entering the building was not without risk.

While the Archons did sleep most of the time, when they did wake, they wandered the halls of Tartarus freely.

Many of Crystal's friends and subordinates had died over the years at the hands of these monsters, despite the Archons' Magic being suppressed, and it looked like they had killed once more. She knew why they did it. She knew what they ate and the power that a Magi's Anima gave them.

But Crystal's mission gave her and her group little choice. They had to monitor these creatures and keep them from meddling too much. It was a balancing act. One that occasionally went wrong.

Crystal reached the body and looked down. It was Warden Drust. He'd been a young Magus and probably not fully prepared to deal with an awake Archon. But none of them should have been awake. They watched them, monitored them, and tried to keep their less experienced members out when one of the Archons was awake. Clearly, they'd got it wrong.

She sighed, mourning the loss of life of another from their ranks.

There were so few of them now.

"If it's any consolation, he died well," said a soft but dangerous, feminine voice.

Crystal looked up and spotted the figure in the shadows, leaning against the pillar. Crystal knew who this was. The swell of her breasts under her cloak, and the smear of blood on her red lips just visible beneath the tattered hood, only confirming what she already knew.

"Not really," Crystal answered. "Why, Lilitu? What are you planning this time?"

The Archon only smiled and receded into the shadows.

Angry, Crystal lifted the body in her arms and marched back out the door. Warden Valen was waiting outside for her, a look of concern on his face. He deflated even more on seeing the body in her arms.

"Which one was it this time?" he asked her.

"Lilitu, she drank his blood."

"Damn. Do we know why they do this?"

Crystal looked up at the Warden, another of the younger guardsmen who was probably unaware of the details. "She'll have consumed his Anima and used the power it gave her to contact a Nomad. We can only guess at their plans and schemes though."

"Their plans?

Crystal nodded. "They're planning something. Something big, I'm sure of it."

"Like what?" he asked as they walked between Tartarus and the Fortress of the Ebon Mark.

"What do all prisoners dream of and plan?"

The Warden seemed to understand and nodded. "Escape."

"God forbid, they ever succeed," Crystal replied, her mind troubled as she thought of the possibilities.

The End

Want a FREE bonus Epilogue Chapter?
Get your free chapter by signing up to my News Letter here:
https://dl.bookfunnel.com/pzayl91f9x

The series continues with Magi Rising, Book 2 of the Magi Saga.
Available here:
http://mybook.to/MagiRising

Author Note

Thank you for reading this book. The Magi Saga and the character of Amanda have been with me for years now, and to finally put her out there as a character of my own is a wonderful and liberating experience.

The earliest recorded iteration of her that I have been able to date is from 1995 when I did a series of sketches of a new superhero character that I called Valkyrie, who had psychic powers. I was very influenced by certain Anime films, like Akira and Geno Cyber at the time, and at one point she even had a cybernetic arm similar to Tetsuo from Akira.

Later, around 1997/98 she was brought into the Role Paying games that I was running with my friends as an NPC (Non-Player Character). She went through several versions of herself during these games, starting off as a mysterious and powerful helper with her friend, Weaver where she had short hair and a cybernetic arm before I changed her to a less powerful magic user who could actually be in the players' party and work with them. It was during this time that her prostitution backstory was developed, as well as her Magical nature.

Later, as she moved into the new millennium, she joined other games, took on her apprentice, Liz and more of her nature was developed, including an important event that will happen at the end of book 4 and continue through book 5. Her hairstyle also changed from short to really short. Maya was introduced, along with Gentle Water and Raven.

Yasmin also appeared around this time, although she went by a different name back then.

Other characters who appeared in the early 2000s were Lucian, Nate, Orion, Xain, Loomis, Celest, Toni, Tabitha, Balor, Horlack, and more.

Finally, in my drawings of her, her hair started to get longer until I made it its current length in 2003, not long before my gaming life drew to a close.

But Amanda just wouldn't go away. I had so many ideas for her, so many stories, that I just had to do something with. That was when the idea of writing a book sprang into my head.

Back then, around 2008-2010, as I was thinking about it and started making plans. I had no idea that Indie publishing would become the thing that it has since become. I discovered Kindle Direct Publishing around 2013 and published book one. Naturally, it didn't do much as I had no idea what to do, and I had no idea you could make a living off this, so I forgot about my book until 2016 when I decided I wanted to create book covers for authors.

In my research, it became clear that you could actually make a living from self-publishing and my determination to make this work returned.

I re-edited book one and re-published it with a new cover and started writing book two.

Since then, I've written the full seven volumes of this series, and started a follow-up series called Star Magi. Book one has also been through several revisions, with this one being the latest.

Thank you for reading Magi Dawn. I really appreciate you joining me on this adventure, and hope you enjoy the books to come.

If you're interested, I have a Facebook Group which you might like to join here;
https://www.facebook.com/groups/MagiSagaFans/

Many Thanks,
Andrew

PS, if you enjoyed this book, don't forget to review it on Amazon. Thank you.

Booklist

For full list of Andrew Dobells Books, visit his website at;
http://www.andrewdobellauthor.co.uk/booklist